# KINGZ OF THE GAME

Playa Ray

Lock Down Publications and Ca$h
Presents
# Kingz of the Game
## A Novel by *Playa Ray*

Playa Ray

# Lock Down Publications
P.O. Box 870494
Mesquite, Tx 75187

**Visit our website @**
www.lockdownpublications.com

**Lock Down Publications**
**Like our page on Facebook: Lock Down Publications @**
www.facebook.com/lockdownpublications.ldp
Cover design and layout by: **Dynasty Cover Me**
Book interior design by:  **Shawn Walker**
Edited by: **Lashonda Johnson**

4

# Stay Connected with Us!

Text **LOCKDOWN** to 22828 to stay up-to-date with new re-
leases, sneak peaks, contests and more…
Or **CLICK HERE** to sign up.
Thank you.

## Like our page on Facebook:

**Lock Down Publications:  Facebook**

**Join** Lock Down Publications/The New Era Reading Group

## Visit our website @
www.lockdownpublications.com

## Follow us on Instagram:

**Lock Down Publications: Instagram**

**Email Us:** We want to hear from you!

# Submission Guideline.

Submit the first three chapters of your completed manuscript to ldpsubmissions@gmail.com, subject line: Your book's title. The manuscript must be in a .doc file and sent as an attachment. Document should be in Times New Roman, double spaced and in size 12 font. Also, provide your synopsis and full contact information. If sending multiple submissions, they must each be in a separate email.

Have a story but no way to send it electronically? You can still submit to LDP/Ca$h Presents. Send in the first three chapters, written or typed, of your completed manuscript to:

LDP: Submissions Dept
Po Box 870494
Mesquite, Tx 75187

*DO NOT send original manuscript. Must be a duplicate.*

Provide your synopsis and a cover letter containing your full contact information.

Thanks for considering LDP and Ca$h Presents.

## ACKNOWLEDGMENTS

*First, I'd like to thank God for blessing me with unlimited talent – even the ones I have yet to discover. Thanks to my lovely grandmother, Mary Robinson for giving birth to my mother, Mary McCoy. Who subsequently had to put up with my mess for a large number of years. To my brothers, Moerise 'Major Gramz' Williams (CEO of Drogue Apparel), Tommy 'Al-Amin'/'Usher' Wright, Michael 'Poppo' Paige, and 'Brother' Raymond Clark. Also, to my sisters, Alicia 'Twin' Flemister and Geneva 'Little Sister' Davis-Moore. I love you all forever! Yes, this also includes you, my adorable niece, Angela 'Angel' Cofer.*

*There were a lot of people supporting me along this journey when my very own family members were incredulous of my ambitions. These people are: Gayla Johnson, Takeisha Thompson, Reginald 'Red' Johnson, Veronica 'T' Thomas, Gordan Futch, Kionte 'Savali Kilumm' Glover, Gabriel 'Detroit Bradley, Jerrod 'Polo' Smith, Latasha M. Brooks, Dartanya 'Dino' Brooks, James 'Tazz' Bennett, Kenneth 'Buster' Hinton, John Priest, Travis 'Trap' Smith, Erlc 'Emo' Swain, Jesse Askews, Randal 'Big Ru' Jones, Blake 'O.P.' Pugh, Wanda 'Nappy Head' Frederick, Demario 'Mario' Gammage, Joe Ross, Lester 'Badi' Parrish, Alvera Fruitrail, Cynthia Stewart, C.V. Walters, Angelo 'Yank G' Greene and Franklin 'Drew' Andrews.*

*As I've asserted there were a lot of people supporting me but, if I resume in this manner, my list would probably take up five or six pages. However, for the ones I did not mention, know this, you are not forgotten. That's on my crown!*

*Other people I'll never forget are Mae McCoy, Kimberly McCoy, J.L. Jones, Tiberius 'T.C.' Hester, Allene 'Pee Wee' Porter, Freeman Sallahuddin, Sister Dyiah Sallahuddin, and Quentin James. To label you all as 'ones I've lost' would be a misnomer, being that I still think of you as if you're still in existence.*

*Last, but not at all least, I want to thank Cash, Shawn Walker, and the staff of Lock Down Publications for all the work they put into this project, and for giving me a chance to 'stomp with the big dogs.'*

*~Playa Ray~*

*"I was once told that people would go too far greater lengths to avoid what they fear than to obtain what they desire. I'm sure you're aware of the 'Game of Thrones' where deception is the art that keeps the world at the king's feet but can also become the sword used to bring him to his knees. Remember, in order to become the dragon slayer, you must, first, slay the dragon."*

*~Kionte 'Savali Kilumm' Glover~*
*Facebook: Savalibigasitgets*

Playa Ray

# CHAPTER 1

## Summer 2002

"Are you gonna give me some money to get my hair fixed?" Kim had entered the kitchen where James was seated at the table, cutting up cocaine on a plate. James was medium-brown, 6'1' and one-hundred and ninety-five pounds, with dark, low-cut wavy hair. He was shirtless, clad in black cargo shorts and Nikes.

If he'd heard Kim, which he did, he made no indications of it, because his back was still to her as he resumed his work. As if ignoring her wasn't enough, he had the audacity to aid *Cee-Lo*, as he sang the chorus to *Eight Ball* and *MJG's 'Paid Dues'* coming from the stereo in the living room.

*"There's a skinny line between wrong and right/trapped in the trap 'til the morning light/ghetto ain't left me no choices, I had to fight/my mom and dad was too young to raise me right—"*

"James!" she interrupted, now standing akimbo. "I know you heard me! I need some money to get my hair fixed!"

That's when he turned in the wooden chair to regard his 5'7' girlfriend, who was wearing low-cut jean shorts, a sleeveless white shirt, and footies. Her bushy hair was combed back like she was attempting to tie it in a ponytail.

"Now, correct me if I'm wrong," he started, "but didn't you get paid yesterday?"

"I also paid the bills yesterday," she retorted. Then she sighed and raised her hands. "You know what? Keep your fucking money, jerk!"

"You better watch your motherfucking mouth!" he said to her back, as she hurried out of the kitchen. He was smiling, but that smile abruptly turned upside down when the stereo went dead. "Man turn my shit back on!" he yelled out.

"Fuck you!" she shot back.

That did it. James was out of his seat, dashing from the kitchen like a bolt of lightning. He didn't even hear the chair as it crashed onto the kitchen floor, but he heard the slam of the bedroom's door, and the clicking of its locks as he neared it.

"Gone, James!" she yelled from the other side.

"You better open this door!" he demanded trying the knob not believing it was locked.

"Ain't!" she responded. "You're not gonna put your hands on me!"

"Hell, you can't stay in there forever!"

"I'll try."

"Why the fuck are you playing with me, Kim?"

"I'm not playing with you," she claimed. "You won't give me no money to get my hair fixed."

"Man fuck your hair!" he spat pointing his index finger at the door like he was pointing directly at her. "I ought to set that shit on fire!"

"You ain't gonna touch my hair!"

"What?"

"You heard me! I don't know what—"

Her words were cut off by the kick James delivered to the door. She let out a shriek. The door didn't give. James was trying to shake her up and remind her who she was dealing with, because, she'd obviously forgotten.

"Kim, you got five seconds to open this door!" he asserted pointing at the door again. "And three of 'em already gone." She didn't respond. "A'ight," he said heading for the kitchen. "I guess I'll shoot through that motherfucker!"

His Glock was on the table, where he'd been cutting up his cocaine. He'd forgotten about the drugs, plus, Ray, his younger brother was on the way to pick him up. He looked at the silver Fossil watch on his arm, it was 12:15 pm. In lieu of his gun, he grabbed the razor disregarding the fallen chair and cut the rest of the white substance into dimes. After placing the rocks into a pill bottle and washing the plate. He was ready to deal with Kim. He put the pill bottle in his pocket, grabbed his gun and set out to do his duty, whatever that was.

He approached the bedroom door again and tapped on it lightly with the barrel of the gun. "Kim?" No answer. "A'ight, Kim," he warned raising his voice a few decibels. "I'm not playing with your stupid ass!" He tried the knob.

It was unlocked, immediately, he was hit with Déjà Vu. He'd been through this before with Kim. Everything was the same, except for the gun.

*He and Kim had got into an argument over her accusations of him cheating on her. Then, as always, she let her mouth defeat her, and she knew it, because as soon as, 'I hope your nasty ass catch AIDS!' rolled off her tongue, she shot from the living room like a bat out of hell. James was sitting on the sofa watching TV when she positioned herself in front of it making her case, gave chase, but he was too slow. She'd already secured herself on the other side of the bedroom door. After what seemed like a century of arguing through the door, James tried a different tack; coaxing.*

*He admitted that he'd only received oral sex from the woman he was accused of, and he was sorry. She was quiet, perhaps listening. He assured her that it wouldn't happen again. She was quiet, perhaps listening. He called her name— he tried the knob. It was unlocked, he'd tricked her. That's when he burst through the door like a raging bull. Eight feet away, Kim stood facing him with her hands behind her back.*

*James advanced on her with no hesitation. All he could manage to get out was, "Bitch, I'm gonna beat—" before her hands came from behind her back, raised into the air.*

*Her left hand was balled into a fist, her right hand wrapped around the handle of a knife. Knife? Where did she get a knife? The kitchen, of course, but when? Why? Was this planned out from the beginning? It had to be. James thought he'd tricked her, but it was obvious she was the one who'd tricked him, he'd walked right into her trap.*

*As he tried to advance, her hands stayed raised mid-air, she let out a loud roar as she hurled, countering his attack. With no time to backpedal, James threw his left arm up in defense. The knife pierced his forearm, he grimaced. Before he knew it, the knife was back in the air. As he anticipated another strike, James couldn't chance that. So, before she could score another point for the home team, he rushed her, grabbed her by the wrist and slammed his body into hers. Using that tactic, he managed to knock the wind out of her, causing her to release the knife and fall to the floor.*

*She breathlessly pleaded for her life, but 'sorry' wouldn't do it. Kim ended up in the hospital with cracked ribs and a fractured jaw. She'd never told anyone what happened to her. That was over a year ago, and they'd had countless fisticuffs since. James and Kim have been lovebirds since high school. When they met James was in the eleventh grade and Kim was in the tenth.*

Now, with his left hand poised on the knob, and his gun in his right, he found himself staring at the scar on his left forearm. The loud sound system of an approaching vehicle brought him out of his trance. *DMX's 'What Them Bitches Want,'* featuring *Sisqo* banged from the speaker. It sounded like the car had stopped in front of the house. James knew it was his brother. He also knew that whatever he was going to do to Kim, he had to do it before Ray came in.

It wasn't that Ray cared about a female getting the dog shit beaten out of her. It was just that Ray and Kim had a sister-brother relationship and James respected that to the fullest. Therefore, he tried not to chastise her in front of him. The music died, and James knew it wouldn't be long before Ray made it to the front door. So, as he left the bedroom door slightly ajar, he took a step back and cocked his gun, injecting a bullet into the chamber.

"Kim?" he called out. "I'm 'bout to come in, plus, I'm strapped. I'm telling you now if you try some bullshit, I'ma light your ass up! That's on everything!"

Without further ado, he kicked the door open, holding the Glock at arm's length with both hands. Kim was not standing in the middle of the room this time. A glance through the crack where the door opened, showed that she wasn't behind the door.

*'Where is she?'* he thought. *'The closet!'*

The closet had double doors that opened in opposite directions. They were closed and in one swift motion, James dashed into the room and kneeled down just long enough to see that Kim wasn't

14

under the bed. Then he stood facing the closet, with his gun trained. Suddenly, he thought he'd heard the front door open. But, it had to be his imagination because they made sure every door was secured before they went to bed at night. Unless Kim had unlocked it, but she didn't have a reason to. Neither one of them had left the house that morning. Therefore, he dismissed the thought and moved slowly towards the closet.

"A'ight, Kim!" he warned, stopping short in front of the closet. "I know your retarded ass is in there."

"Who are you talking to, James?"

Kim's voice – which did not come from the closet – startled him, causing him to turn abruptly towards the door, aiming his gun. She was standing in the doorway, smiling, with her arm around Ray's waist, while he stood with his arm over her shoulder.

Ray was two years younger than James, he was light-skinned, 5'10' and one-hundred and sixty pounds. He was clad in Khaki shorts, a white *Polo* shirt, and white low-cut *K-Swiss* shoes. His hair was braided to the back and concealed under his white *Kangol* hat. He was regarding James through gold-rimmed sunglasses. Apparently, Kim had eased out the door when James made his journey back to the kitchen. Now she was safe, she always felt safe when her *'big brother'*, as she called him, even though she was one year older than him, came around.

"Now, I've heard of people having skeletons in the closet," Ray spoke. "But I didn't think they were actually in the closet."

"Go to hell!" James said, smiling. He tucked the gun in the front of his shorts, then spoke to Kim. "I'ma whoop your ass!"

"I haven't done anything to you!"

"You keep playing with me!"

"Man, we gonna ride or what?" Ray intervened. "I told, Black, I was gonna scoop him up too."

"Yeah, let me get right," James responded and moved around the room.

First, he put on a black t-shirt that was lying on the bed. Then he retrieved his cell phone and necklace from the nightstand beside the bed, then put the phone in his pocket and the necklace around his neck.. The letter 'J' hung from the chain down to his stomach. He pulled a wad of bills from the drawer and approached them. "Two hundred, right?"

"Yes," Kim answered like a small child as she and Ray withdrew their arms from around each other.

"I'll fuck around and go broke fucking with you and your nappy ass hair!" he stated flipping through the bills.

Then he eyed her silently daring her to say something smart, but it wouldn't have mattered. He was going to give her the money anyway because, as his girl, she represented him. If she looked bad, then he looked bad, and vice versa.

"Thank you," she said counting the money to make sure he didn't trick her again.

Once James had retrieved his black fitted cap from the closet, he and Ray were out the door headed for Ray's black four-door '85 Delta Eighty-Eight. James was already in the front passenger seat with his gun in his lap, looking through Ray's CD case, before Ray could circle around. As he slid into the driver's seat, Ray pulled his black .380 from its holster and placed it in his lap while James ejected DMX and inserted another disc.

"Who told you to take my shit out?" Ray asked.

"Man, you know, I gotta hear my boy," James replied. "And when are you gonna put this motherfucker in the game?"

"Hell, I can barely keep this shit running, but I got B.J. on the lookout for some rims," Ray replied.

Ray started the car and James selected a track on the CD. They pulled off as *Bone Crusher's 'Never Scared'* roared through the four 6x9s on the back deck, and two 12s in the trunk. Ray entered Capital Homes and pulled up to Black's apartment. Black must have heard the music before Ray turned it down because he was coming out of his apartment as the metal screen door slammed behind him. Black was dark-skinned, medium height, and about one-hundred and seventy pounds. He was clad in a blue *Sean Jean* shorts set, matching shoes, and carrying a blue hat. He climbed in behind James.

"Match one," James told him.

"You got the blunts?" Black asked.

"Nah," he answered, then looked at Ray. "Stop by a gas station."

Playa Ray

## CHAPTER 2

On the west side of Atlanta, Maddox Park was quite packed as Ray entered riding slowly behind a line of vehicles that were moving at a snail's pace. The sun was blazing, women were walking around in the skimpiest outfits, the men were dressed to impress, children were being children, a few grills were in effect, the swimming pool was packed and loud music was coming from vehicles and portable radios.

Ray pulled off to the right parking behind another line of cars. James and Black had individual blunts rolled up, which they immediately fired up upon dismounting since Ray didn't smoke and wouldn't allow it in his car. Ray perched up on the left side of the hood, enjoying his bag of Doritos and 20-ounce Sprite. James was sitting on the front end of the hood, and Black was leaned against the driver's door. They relished their blunts and beers.

"Man, y'all wouldn't believe who I saw at Body Tap last night," Black spoke, taking a sip of his beer.

"What the hell were you doing at the Tap?" James questioned.

"That bitch, Felicia," Black stated disregarding James' query.

"Your baby mama?" Ray asked.

"You mean *one* of his baby mamas?" James corrected, being that Black had four children by three women.

"Tell me she was getting a lap dance," Ray insisted.

"Hell nah!" Black regarded Ray. "She was *giving* a lap dance."

"Oh, yeah?" James asked as a smile played across his face. "She gonna be there tonight?"

Black stared at James with a blank expression. Ray saw it and couldn't suppress his laughter. He and James were rolling, Black just shook his head, swallowed the rest of his beer and tossed the can under the car.

"Man don't start that ol' sentimental shit!" James voiced.

"Yeah," Ray joined in. "We're not trying to see your baby mama naked."

"Hold on!" James protested. "I didn't say all that."

They were rolling again. Without a word, Black crossed the road and approached three women.

"What the hell is this nigga up to?" James asked as he came around the car and leaned against the driver's door.

"Ain't no telling," Ray answered, placing the empty drink bottle into the empty chip bag.

"Put this in there," James handed him the beer can as he kept his eyes on Black, who was still confabbing with the trio.

Ray cut between cars as he crossed the street to the trash can, then doubled back, taking his spot on the hood. They saw that Black and his new-found friends were coming their way.

"These are my folks, James and Ray," Black was telling the girls. "Y'all this is Connie, Meeka, and Sylvia."

James struck up a conversation with Meeka, seeing that Black had already laid claim to Connie. Sylvia positioned herself in front of Ray, smiling. She was dark-skinned, 5'8', with short hair. Her short, jean skirt hugged her wide hips, while her full breasts threatened to burst through her blue sleeveless shirt. She moved closer and leaned slightly forward, with her face just inches away from his, like she was analyzing a statue.

"I can't see your eyes," she proclaimed, her breath smelling of peppermint.

"You're not supposed to," he countered.

"You must be high?"

"Nope."

"Shy?"

"Yep."

"Oh!" She straightened her pose but kept her eyes on him. "I like my men shy."

"Oh, yeah?" Ray inquired.

"Mmm-hmm." She bit down on her bottom lip.

"And what do you do with shy men?"

She leaned forward and whispered in his ear. "Whatever they want me to do."

Her extremely soft lips brushed his ear as she spoke, triggering something inside him. Ray was highly turned on but knew he had to maintain his composure.

"Shawty, I'm not looking for a relationship," he managed to get out.

"That makes two of us," she responded. "I just like to have fun. How 'bout you?"

"The same."

"Can we exchange digits?"

"Yeah, we can make that move."

While she was rummaging through her purse for a pen and some paper, James' cell phone rang, it was Fred. He wanted the crew to rendezvous at his place, so, after exchanging numbers with the women, they were ready to migrate. As they were about to climb in the car, they saw a line of convertibles, ranging from Mustangs, Benzes, Lexus', Jaguars, and Cadillac XLR's pull into the park.

"I should've known *they* were gonna ride through," James asserted standing by the passenger's door.

The first car, a red Ford Mustang, stopped in front of Ray, who was still standing at the driver's door. There were two men occupying it. They were wearing gold necklaces with large medallions that read: *Drop Squad.* They were known from Atlanta to wherever for drugs, robbery, murder, you name it! Like a Mafia, they were notorious and *'plenty deep.'*

"You gotta step it up, pimpin'!" the passenger said to Ray.

"Nigga, why the fuck is you worried 'bout our shit?" James spat from the other side of the car.

He already hated these niggas with a passion. Plus, he woke up every morning praying that a nigga would get out of pocket, so he could wreck some shit. The passenger laughed, apparently amused by James comment. Ray disregarded the passenger and looked over at his brother hoping like hell James didn't amplify the situation, knowing how aggressive he was at times. He didn't think before he acted, but when he did act, he would take on a whole nation.

To James, there was no such thing as *'odds.'* It was all even! That's why Ray respected his brother to the fullest. He may not have coincided with a lot of James' antics, but he was ready to ride whenever the time came. So, if it was going down, then it was going all the way down. Fuck the odds!

"My bad pimp!" the passenger said to James, raising his hands in mock surrender. "We ain't looking for no trouble." He then motioned for his driver to move on.

They watched as the line proceeded on, every occupant sported the *'Drop Squad'* emblem. When the show was over, they climbed into the Delta.

"You need to step your whip game up," James told Ray.

Ray looked at his brother. "That's if you don't get me killed before I get a chance to."

# CHAPTER 3

Ray was driving his car through Howell Station – also known as Knight Park – where they used to roam before moving into their own places. Although James and Ray stayed in Bland Town, and Black stayed in the Bluff, they spent most of their time in Knight Park. There were all kinds of houses: shabby, run-down, modern, and a few antediluvians that had withstood the tests of time. It was a nice, quiet, and desegregated neighborhood. The crew had even witnessed the Fulton County Jail being built right next to their locality that was partitioned by a razor-wire fence.

Ray pulled up in front of Fred's house which was a bit shabby and parked behind Fred's gray, four-door, '84 Oldsmobile Cutlass. Fred still lived with his mother by choice. He didn't have his own place, because he couldn't stand leaving his mother alone in that house, being that she was old and couldn't manage much, like the bills and groceries, which Fred and his older brother Eric took care of.

The front door was open and as they approached, they saw Fred sitting in the living room, talking to his mother. Fred had high-yellow colored skin, stood 5'11', and weighed one hundred and sixty-five pounds. He was twenty-four years old, the same age as James, and wore his hair cut low.

Seeing them at the door, Fred motioned for them to enter. After making their greetings to his mother, they followed Fred to his room. Fred locked the door as Ray and Black sat on the sofa, and James leaned against the dresser.

"I went shopping," Fred announced, crossing the room to the closet.

They knew exactly what he was talking about. The closet resembled a mini arsenal. It held more guns than clothes. Fred pulled out a pistol-grip pump and handed it to James. James face lit up like a child on Christmas as he admired the tool. Fred then handed Ray and Black analogous AK-47s.

"They're loaded," Fred warned as he pulled out another pistol-grip kin to the one James held and sat on the arm of the sofa.

"So, what'cha got in mind?" asked James.

"Tee told me she's pregnant," Fred replied.

"So, we just go over there and shoot the baby out of her?" Ray asked.

"Abortion clinic making house calls?" James replied amused. "I like that shit!"

Fred laughed. "Y'all are some real late-night comedians!"

"I'm in," said Black. "As long as we can stop by Felicia's house, too."

That tickled Ray and James and Black joined in. When James saw that Fred didn't get the joke, he explained that Black was upset about encountering his son's mother at a strip club. Fred smiled, his friends never failed to amuse him. This was his circle. At that moment, somebody tapped on the window. Fred turned and drew back the curtains of the open window. It was one of his customers trying to acquire two dimes. Since Fred hadn't done his re-up yet, he let James catch the sale.

"Man, this shits not booming like it used to," Fred declared, once the customer left. "If a nigga ain't moving weight, he ain't really gonna see no real money."

"So, who do we hit first?" James asked, picking up on the hint.

Fred looked at him, then to his other confidants. Before he could convey what was on his mind, his mother called him from the living room.

"Ma'am?" he answered.

"You have more company," she announced.

"Man, I hope one of these hoes ain't just popped up on me like that." He placed the pump back into the closet. "I'll be back," he told them, leaving the room only to return seconds later. "Ray, that's B.J. he done stole somebody's Benz."

"Straight up?" Ray stood, relinquishing the AK to Fred.

"Hell yeah," Fred replied. "And it's sitting up!"

Ray laughed as he exited the room. Fred locked the door back.

"So, who do we hit first?" James rehashed.

"I'll tell you when Ray gets back," Fred told him.

"You might as well come on with it," James insisted. "He won't be in on this one."

"Why not?"

"I'm excluding him."

"Why?"

"Because I'm his big brother and I have a right to do that."

"I'm quite sure he's trying to get his paper right, too," Fred pointed out.

"I'll make sure he's straight."

They stared at each other.

"Look—" James broke the silence. "—I don't want him involved just in case shit don't go right."

"A'ight," Fred gave in. He sat on the bed, placing the AK beside him. "I ain't mapped everything out yet."

\*\*\*

When Ray got outside, B.J. was standing in the front yard. He was light-skinned, 5'9', one-hundred and seventy pounds, and stocky. He was originally from East Lake Meadows, with family in Bland Town, where he used to spend his summers when he was younger. That's how he and Ray had met. They were tight from then on. They'd even started regarding each other as 'cousins.'

"What's up, boy?" B.J. greeted him.

"What the move is?"

They dapped.

"I can't call it," B.J. answered. "How much weed you got on you?"

"Six more twenties."

"Let me get 'em," he insisted. "I'll straighten you out when I drop the Benz off."

'*The Benz!*' That's when Ray spotted it. It was black, with tinted windows and chrome wheels. There were two guys – B.J.'s car thief buddies – and three, young looking girls standing by it. B.J. was eighteen-years-old, so the girls had to be somewhere in that vicinity, but the car was eminently familiar to him.

"Whose car is that?" Ray asked, looking B.J. in the face, knowing he would lie to God.

"The hell if I know!" answered BJ. "Why?"

"I've seen it somewhere," Ray spoke as if he was trying to retain.

B.J. told Ray how they'd procured the car. They pulled into a gas station in another *'hot box,'* and spotted the Benz still running. Considering they would get more money for the Benz than the car, they'd pulled up in, they made their decision.

"Man ditch that car!" Ray said, heading for his car.

"I am," B.J. said, following behind him. "I can't just fall off in the chop shop. You know how the twins operate, appointments. Mines at twelve tonight."

Climbing into the driver's seat of his car, Ray pulled a large Ziploc bag from under the seat. He pulled a bag of weed from the bag, stuffed it in the ashtray, then handed the Ziploc to B.J.

"That's five," he told B.J. "Now go and park that damn car!"

"Yes, sir!" B.J. was smiling. "Anything else Captain?"

"Be careful!"

"Come on, Ray!" B.J. lifted his shirt, revealing the handle of his gun. "I stay strapped!"

"A lot of niggas die strapped."

"A'ight Malcolm X," B.J. clowned. "We're about to hit the hotel, bust these hoes up, drop these hoes off, and get paid."

Ray asked. "And how old are *'these hoes'?*"

"Grown," he answered, heading for the car. "One!"

"One!" Ray responded, which signified *'One love.'*

Then, Fred, James, and Black emerged from the house.

"Somebody's gonna fuck around and knock y'all asses off 'bout their shit!" Fred yelled out to B.J. and his crew as they climbed into the Benz and sped away.

"So, what the move is?" Ray asked as his crew approached.

"Shit find something to get into," Fred answered.

"I need to re-up first," Ray asserted.

"Eric ain't doing nothing until tomorrow," Fred reported. "Right now, we're about to hit that downtown. You in?"

"You know I'm in."

"You ain't got no more dope, Ray?" James asked.

"I got one more bag."

James turned to Black. "Match one?"

"Hell yeah!"

They both gave Ray ten dollars.

"Roll 'em up," James told Black.

James climbed into the car with Fred, and Black rode with Ray, rolling only two blunts for he and James since Fred just like Ray didn't smoke either.

\*\*\*

Once they got downtown, they parked in the parking garage and walked around. Downtown Atlanta was packed as always with people moving about, working, shopping, eating, and just enjoying themselves. This was a regular hang-out spot for a lot of people. It was much better than the mall and a real tourist attraction.

Then, they journeyed through Underground Atlanta, making it to the food court, where a line of built-in-wall restaurants was. The aroma of various foods flooded the environment. The crew opted for Long John Silvers and copped a table.

"So what'cha gonna do about, Tee?" Black asked Fred.

"Abortion," he uttered.

"Shawty's crazy about you," James interjected. "She's not going for that shit!"

"She ain't got no choice!" Fred snapped.

"Why not?"

"Because it's not mine."

"Come on Casanova!" James persisted. "We stopped shooting dog water at nine. Unless you're barren."

"I know you didn't!" Fred countered, laughing. "You and Kim have been together way before Moses parted the Red Sea and still ain't got no children."

"You know why?"

"Cause you got your tubes tied?" Fred offered.

James was so tickled he couldn't muster a response. "Man, I gotta piss!" he declared, standing. "We gotta hit that arcade later, too."

Apparently, Black had to go also because he was right behind James.

"So, what did I miss?" Ray asked Fred.

"What'cha mean?"

"Back at the house."

"Oh!"

Fred would never lie to his trues. He would also never betray, nor break a promise to them, which was why at the moment, he was stuck between a rock and a hard place. He had assured James that he wouldn't disclose their plot to Ray. Although Fred had explained to James that they may need a fourth man, James still refused to include Ray.

"Just chill," Fred told Ray. "When it goes down, you'll know."

James and Black had emerged from the restroom. James stopped to converse with a female, who was standing around like she was waiting on someone. Black continued to the table.

"What's up, shawty?" James greeted her.

"Hey," she responded.

"Where you from?" he asked.

"Adamsville."

"Shawty, you ain't up out that ADV!" James said smiling.

"Who ain't!" she retorted, smiling back. "I rep my hood to the fullest!"

"Say, homeboy?" a man's voice intercepted. "You're barking up the wrong tree!"

Three men had approached from the right of James. He turned and faced the one who'd spoken, apparently, he was the girl's boyfriend.

"Says who?" James demanded, ready to receive his blessing.

# CHAPTER 4

Ray spotted James and Black when they loomed from the restroom. James stopped to talk to some girl, while Black came back to the table. Due to past experiences whenever they enter crowded areas and someone branched off, Ray kept an eye out for the stragglers, just in case.

Now, watching his brother from across the vast room, he saw three goons approach him. James turned to face-off with one of them. Ray couldn't see James' face, but he could see the face of the guy James was swapping words with. As soon as the guy looked James up and down, sizing him up, James' hand moved in a lightning motion. The slap echoed like a firecracker through the crowded and noisy room.

Fred was watching the scene as well. As soon as James struck, he and Ray simultaneously lunged from their chairs and dashed towards the site, with Black right behind them. James was now going toe-to-toe with the trio, taking more licks, then he conduced. People had stopped what they were doing to scrutinize the brawl.

As they neared, Fred and Black tucked their chains inside their shirts, and Ray stuffed his sunglasses in his pocket. The goons didn't know it was about to get ugly for them until it was too late. Fred caught one of them with a blow to the chin, knocking him out. Ray planted his foot into the second guy's ribs like he was kicking a door in. He yelled out in pain as the blow knocked him sideways off his feet.

Black attacked the third guy with a hail of blows to the face, drawing blood from his nose and mouth. The guy immediately surrendered, after accepting that the tables had turned, his friends were on the ground, one asleep and the other was clutching his side.

Someone yelled, "Security!"

That's when they looked to see Underground security moving in on their left. To their right was a pair of double doors. It was either go to jail or run, they opted for the latter. They burst through the doors leading to another part of Underground Atlanta and accessed the parking garage. Then they hiked up the stairs to the level they'd parked on. After making it to the cars they paused to inspect each other. James' lip was bleeding but the rest were un-scathed.

\*\*\*

It was after 9 p.m. when Ray pulled up to James' house. After leaving downtown they all journeyed back to Knight Park. Like Fred had mentioned, the trap wasn't booming the way it used to. So, James and Ray migrated to Bland Town, where they'd grown up and their mother still resided. They stopped by her house, but she wasn't home. So, they hung out until James sold the rest of his prod-uct.

"I don't know why I asked you to bring me home this early," James now said, regarding his house that had no lights on inside. "I need some pussy, and Kim's stupid ass don't get off until eleven."

Ray just listened.

"I might go fuck, Brenda."

"Brenda!" Ray exclaimed.

"Hell yeah!"

"Didn't Kim try to kill you about, Brenda?" Ray asked, refer-ring to the incident when Kim had adopted the persona of the '*Bride of Chucky*.'

"You ain't never got no head from, Brenda?"

"Nah."

"I can tell."

"How's that?"

"Cause you ain't never mentioned it," James pointed out. "That's all niggas talk about whenever somebody mentions her. That fire head, she'll make a nigga leave his whole family!"

After dropping James off at Brenda's house, five houses down from James' house. Ray headed for his apartment. For some reason, he started thinking about the girl he'd met at the park earlier. He couldn't remember her name, but she'd written it on the non-win-ning scratch-off ticket in his pocket. The girl was fine, she was dark-skinned and thick in all the right places. Her lips were soft and lus-cious. He wondered if she had the power to make a man leave his whole family. Now, he was feeling like his brother, he needed some!

What James said about Brenda had to be true, because he'd overheard many guys praise her '*mouth service.*' He'd even heard some dudes talking about her this past, Easter, at church!

So, why hadn't he sampled the goodies? Ray didn't have an an-swer for that. He tried to censor his indecent thoughts and think about something else, but it was futile. After all, it's been over two weeks since his last rendezvous. It was a one-night stand, in fact, it was a hook-up through his childhood buddy, B.J.

*'B.J. where the hell was B.J.? He was in that Benz, that damn familiar looking ass Benz!'* This shit really irked, Ray because he'd had a bad vibe from the moment he laid eyes on the car, but where the hell had he seen this car? There weren't too many Mercedes Benzes customarily parallel on this side of town.

*'Think Ray, think, that's it!'* Ray and the crew were in East Point, at the bowling alley almost a month ago. The car had entered the parking lot, just as they were exiting the building. Fascinated by Benzes, Ray watched the car as it parked two cars away from his. It was all coming back to him now. Two guys emerged from the car. Ray wasn't that good at remembering faces, although, these guys' faces were unimportant at the time, there was something ex-ceedingly noticeable about them— their chains.

"Damn!" Ray pulled his cell phone from his hip and dialed B.J.'s number as he drove.

The phone beeped for the umpteenth time today, indicating that the battery was low. He'd disposed of his car charger yesterday due to a shortage in the cord. Then to make matters more difficult, he'd forgotten to charge the phone last night.

"Yeah?" B.J.'s voice came through.

"Man, where y'all at?" Ray demanded.

"At the hotel. Why?"

*Beep!*

"Which one?"

"Days Inn."

"Where's the car?"

"Um—" B.J. hesitated, then spoke to someone in the background.

*Beep!*

"Lil Dave and one of the girls went to Krystal's," B.J. responded. "Why, what's up?"

"When they get back, park that car and don't get back in it!"

"Man, it's ten fifteen," B.J. complained. "When we drop the—"

*Beep!*

"Hello?" Ray yelled into the dead phone. "B.J.!"

Ray tossed the phone on the passenger's seat. He didn't even get a chance to tell B.J. about the damn car! He wondered if B.J. had recognized the warning in his tone. He had to, but knowing B.J., he was going to get that car over the finish line, even if he had to push it. Fuck who the car belonged to! Ray knew which Days Inn they were holed up in because they always used it. He also knew his friend's life was in danger, and there was nothing he could do about it. Or was there? He was the only one who'd always been able to talk B.J. out of his mischievous acts before they were committed, but it was always done face-to-face.

\*\*\*

Eric was sitting on his porch when Fred pulled into the driveway and parked behind his black Chevy Caprice. The porch light was off, so Eric was sitting in the dark, wearing dark clothing with his shoulder holster on that conveyed two, .44 Desert Eagles. Two of his pit bulls lay at his feet. Eric was brown-skinned, 6'2', and wore his hair braided to the back. At the age of twenty-seven, he was faring well.

He cooked his own cocaine and grew his own marijuana. His clientele was small including Fred and his crew, but he was doing more numbers than most of his colleagues in the game. At any time,

Fred could team up with his brother as business partners, but he deemed that a man should make his own money—no hand-outs!

"War in the Middle East?" Fred asked as he sat up on the porch railing, being that Eric occupied the only chair.

"Always," he answered.

"Who's on your list this time?"

"Curt."

"Hell, he's always on your list," Fred snickered. "Late again, huh?"

"Yeah." Eric took a drag on his blunt that Fred hadn't noticed. "As soon as I find another runner, I'ma fire his ass."

"What you think he be doing?"

"Tricking off. That's his business, but he's doing it on my time."

Fred was quiet, Eric pulled on his blunt. "Gone and get you a chair out the kitchen," Eric said.

"Nah, I'm straight, bruh," Fred protested. "I'm really just passing through."

"It ain't like you to just be passing through," Eric knowingly stated. "What's on your mind?"

After seconds of hesitation, Fred spoke. "I put the crew on to the lick."

"And they turned it down," Eric assumed.

"Not really, James and Black agreed to it, but James don't want Ray involved."

"Why not?"

"Just in case shit don't go right," he says.

"He's worried about his lil' brotha," Eric asserted. "That's typical."

"Hell, I worry about you, but I know you're tough as fuck!" Eric stated.

They sat in silence while Eric finished his blunt. "So, Ray agreed with that shit?" Eric finally asked.

"He doesn't know about it."

There was another moment of silence.

"Y'all still might need a fourth man," Eric stated. "At least I think so. To be on the safe side."

"Yeah! I think so too."

## CHAPTER 5

Ray pulled into the Days Inn parking lot and circled the perimeter. There was no sign of the Benz. He was wishing he'd gotten the room number before the phone disconnected. He found a spot and parked. Surely, he couldn't go from door to door looking for someone else's bad-ass children, but what if they'd already left? He thought about driving out to the chop shop he and B.J. used to cash in stolen cars, and ask the twins if they'd been through?

"Nah, definitely not!" he said aloud shaking his head. "That would be too much driving for one night."

At that moment, Ray heard the sound system of a vehicle as it pulled into the lot. He looked back as it rode by, the Benz! He inserted his gun into its holster and dismounted. Noticing that the car was parked about seven cars up, he headed in that direction. That's when he saw five men emerge from a black Chevy Celebrity that was parked across the lot from the Benz. Lil Dave and the girl got out, gathering bags of food from the car. The men were headed in their direction.

Ray stopped in his tracks. Not because they out-numbered him. Not because they were all carrying handguns, but because he was too late, and he didn't need a psychic to tell him what was about to transpire, or who the men were. Their jewelry told it all.

Apparently, the predators didn't detect Ray as they approached their prey. One of them yelled, "Hey!" Getting the kids attention.

Then, instantaneously, their guns raised. Ray saw the apprehension in the kid's eyes before the guns erupted, and bullets tore through them. Breaking out of his trance, Ray ducked between cars, pulling his pistol. The gunfire ceased, but it wasn't over yet, because they were still out there, and Ray wasn't one hundred percent sure if they'd seen him. This was a notorious group, known for eliminating and evaporating without a trace. To overlook a witness would be an amateur's mistake and these guys were no amateurs!

Ray heard the slamming of car doors. Seconds later, the Benz, followed by the Chevy, sped by racing out of the parking lot. He realized he was holding his breath and exhaled. As he got up from his crouching position, he quickly holstered his weapon, as people started coming out of their rooms.

*\*\*\**

Ray was awakened by the pounding on his door. He rolled over and glanced at the clock on the nightstand it was 8:47 a.m. Any other time, he would've been upset to be disturbed at this time of the morning. But, right now, he felt a bit relieved to be rescued from the appalling nightmare he was having. He dreamed he'd witnessed one of B.J.'s proteges and a young girl, both sixteen-years-old being gunned down by Drop Squad.

"Who is it?" Ray approached the door clad in a pair of boxer shorts and a t-shirt.

"B.J.," his friend answered.

Ray opened the door, the look on B.J.'s face brought Ray back to reality. It wasn't a nightmare after all. He'd actually, witnessed this tragedy.

"Come on in," he told B.J.

B.J. entered and they sat at the kitchen table. Neither one spoke for a while. "You a'ight?" Ray finally asked.

"Yeah," he answered, reluctant to make eye contact. "I told them I was gonna grab some food, but Dave begged me to let him go. Hell, he had bugged me all day about driving the Benz."

Ray asked, "Do you blame yourself?"

Now B.J. stared at him. "Shit, it's my fault! Had I never let him drive—"

"Then you would've been their target," Ray cut in. "I'm not saying what they did was right, but they felt somebody had to pay, they retaliated. Ain't no rules when it comes to that. *anybody* can stand-in for a primary target. That's what happened to Tracey's mom."

"What'cha mean?"

"She was messing with some dude from Drop Squad, remember?"

"Yeah, some dude named, Rico."

"Well, Tracey stole money from, Rico," Ray informed. "Close to a hundred thousand. She got ghost, but she made one big mistake.

"She left her mom behind," B.J. filled in.

Ray nodded.

"I wonder what she's doing now?"

"She's dead."

"Yeah?"

"She came to the funeral," Ray told him. "Later that night, they found her in a dumpster. After they put the fire out.

"Damn!"

"I know, but like I said, ain't no rules in retaliation."

"I still feel bad about the lil homie and ole girl," B.J. admitted.

"That's normal," Ray assured him. "I shouldn't have to sit here and preach the game to you. You already know the pros and cons of it. Hell, I hate I even introduced you to the shit."

"So, if something happens to me," B.J. asked. "You'll feel like it's your fault?"

"Of course, I'll feel like it is," Ray answered. "But deep down inside, I'll know it's not my fault. Not only did I teach you how to steal and make money off cars. I educated you on how dangerous it is. Am I right?"

"Yeah, you're right," he answered. "But which one would you consider more dangerous? Selling dope or stealing cars?"

"You're asking me that because I've done both?"

"Yeah."

"I guess I feel more danger selling dope than I did when we were stealing cars," Ray answered.

"I thought so," B.J. stood, pulled a wad of bills from his pocket, peeled off a crisp one-hundred-dollar bill and held it out to Ray, who just stared at it. "For the weed," B.J. reminded.

"If you need it, keep it."

"I'm straight," B.J. said. "We lost the Benz, but the Chrysler was still at the gas station."

Ray accepted the money.

B.J. asked, "You're gonna re-up today, right?"

"Yeah."

"When you do, hit me up."

"I'll do that," Ray promised. "What you about to get into at nine in the morning?"

"The bed," B.J. announced. "I told Krystal I was on my way. Don't forget to hit me up."

"No doubt." Ray stood up. "You just be careful."

They hugged and B.J. made his exit.

Although he was tired, Ray could not bring himself to resume his slumber. He just couldn't stop thinking about last night's shooting. He'd always heard about kids losing their lives at a young age, but to witness it first-hand, was a whole different ball game, and for what, a car?

After soaking in the tub for almost two hours, Ray ate breakfast, then cleaned up his apartment. He came across his cell phone that he'd forgotten to charge again, then he remembered that he needed to buy a new phone charger for the car, that would be the first thing on his 'to do' list for today.

*** 

"Damn," James said his voice void of emotion after Ray gave him the run-down of last night's event. He was seated in the front passenger seat of Ray's car, rolling a blunt. "You shouldn't have gone out there by yourself, though. What if they'd seen you?"

"Hell, it would've gone down," Ray responded. "They ain't bulletproof!"

"They damn sure act like it," Black said from the back seat.

"You know how I'm looking at that shit, right?" James asked Ray.

Ray knew but didn't respond.

"That stupid ass nigga almost got you killed!"

"I went down there on my own!" Ray stood his ground.

"To save his life and almost got yours taken."

Ray drove in silence, to advance this argument would be futile, considering the hatred James always had for B.J. He believed B.J. would be Ray's downfall or the one to kill him.

Ray parked in front of Eric's house. Fred had agreed to meet them there, so his car was already in the driveway behind Eric's. James and Black fired up blunts upon dismounting.

"Where'd you get this weed from?" Black asked James as they neared the house.

"Why?" James asked, reluctant to answer. To do so would reveal his rendezvous with Brenda. It's not like he didn't trust Black. It was just that he preferred to keep some things concealed.

"Cause, this shits stale!" Black complained.

"That's just like a nigga!" James spat. "Always complaining about some free shit! You wanna pay me for it?"

"Hell nah!"

Eric had stepped out onto the porch with a small, folded paper bag in his hand that he handed to James. He told Ray and Black, Fred would assist them with their orders inside and told James he needed to have a word with him.

"So, what'd you think about the lick?" Eric asked once they were alone.

"We haven't cased it out yet," James answered. "But, I'm in."

Eric nodded. "I've heard, I also heard you excluded, Ray."

"I don't want him in on it."

"I feel that," Eric confirmed. "That's your lil' brotha. Fred's my lil' brotha. I don't want him doing this shit, but I know he's trained to go. Plus, had I not put y'all on to it, y'all would've found one anyway." James just listened. "Y'all are trying to get it up and I respect that," Eric continued. "It's a sweet lick, but I think it's gonna take all four of y'all unless y'all find a substitute for, Ray."

"Shit, I'm two niggas by myself!" James boasted. "I'll pick up all the slack."

"It should be enough money and dope to set all four of y'all straight."

"It's not about the money, E!" James insisted.

"You don't think he could pull something like this off?" Eric guessed.

"It's not that," James said. "Shit might take a wrong turn. We might have to bust our guns. Ray ain't built for that type of shit."

"That's what I thought about, Fred."

## CHAPTER 6

"Are y'all gonna pick me up when I get off?" Kim asked from the back seat of Ray's car as he pulled into Burger King's parking lot. She'd called James while he was talking to Eric and informed him that her friend's car had mechanical issues and she needed a ride to work.

"Yeah, we'll scoop you up," Ray told her.

"Thank you, big brotha!"

"No doubt."

As she got out, she leaned through the passenger window and kissed James in the mouth. "I'll see y'all later," she said, then headed inside.

"Awww, that's so sweet!" Ray teased pulling off.

"Oh, don't hate!"

"Why would I do that?" Ray replied. "I love watching *'What's Love Got to Do Wit' It*."

Ignoring his brother, James answered his vibrating cell phone. "What's up?"

"Is this James?" a female's voice asked.

"Yeah, who's this?"

"You don't remember the women you give your number to?"

"Not really."

"Well, you met me at the park yesterday."

"Oh yeah, what up, Meeka?"

"Nothing," she answered. "What'cha doing?"

"I'm on my way to my mom's crib for Sunday dinner."

"What about afterward?"

"I gotta handle a few affairs. Why?"

She explained that she was bored and in need of company. It sounded good to him, but Sunday dinner with their mother was a ritual. It was always James, Ray, April, and their mother, until their younger sister was accepted at Harvard University in Massachusetts. As much as James wanted to go over to Meeka's place and give her *'the business,'* he had to take a rain check.

\*\*\*

"Mark called me a few minutes ago," Their mother told Ray after she'd opened the door and hugged them both.

Mary was 5'5, with auburn red hair, which she had parted in the middle and pulled tightly into a bun. Today the forty-three-year-old, light-skinned woman's face was adorned with a light application of foundation and red lipstick. As a woman of Christianity, she was clad in one of her many Sunday dresses.

"What'd you cook?" Ray asked trying to avoid a conversation about people he cared nothing about. Mark was his dad unless she was referring to his half-brother, whose name was also Mark.

"Meatloaf, dressing, cornbread, cabbages, black-eyed peas and mashed potatoes," Mary answered.

"Mama, that's a whole banquet!" James voiced. "You got somebody else coming over?"

She said, "I invited my friend."

"What friend?" they both demanded in unison, knowing she was talking about a man.

They were already in defense mode, being that the man she'd dated when they were younger, had ruined her life by introducing her to crack cocaine. He didn't stay around long enough for them to remember his name. She'd been clean for over nine months now, and they were very proud of her. So, there was no way in hell they were going to let another man or woman stress her to the point of relapsing.

"His name is, Robert," she told them.

"I ain't never heard of him," James said. "How 'bout you Ray?"

"Never."

"How long have you been knowing this clown?" James asked.

"A month and a half," his mother replied.

"And why haven't you told us about this clown?" Ray asked.

"He's not a clown," she defended.

"Why haven't you told us about this clown, mama?" James re-iterated Ray's question.

"Because I knew y'all were gonna act like this," she responded, pouting and crossing her arms over her chest.

"Oh, you ain't seen nothing yet!" James warned. "If he's more than two years younger than you, you might as well fix him a doggy-bag, cause he ain't coming in here!"

Mary looked at Ray as if she was waiting for him to defend her since he'd always been more reasonable than James, but Ray just returned her stare with no objections to James' statement.

***

"I tow cars for *Triple-A Towing*," Robert answered another one of James interrogative questions.

James was seated across the table from Robert, eyeing him like a hawk ready to attack at any moment. Robert already had two strikes against him. Number one was that he was dating their mother. Number two he was only forty-years-old, which made him three years younger than her. Lucky for him, Ray had talked James into overlooking the age difference for their mother's sake. Plus, that gave them a chance to interrogate him properly. Good cop, bad cop style!

"You tow cars?" James asked in disgust, casting a glance at his mother.

She was sitting beside Robert, looking down at her food, making designs in her mashed potatoes, obviously agitated by the way her son was behaving.

"That's a decent job," Ray asserted.

"Thanks," said Robert. "I'm also the shop's mechanic."

"You wanna compliment him on that, too?" James asked Ray who was seated beside him.

"How long have you been there?" Ray asked Robert ignoring his brother.

"I've been there for over seventeen years."

James intervened, "How much do you make?"

"James, that is none of your business!" their mother came alive.

"You got two choices," James told Robert. "You can either answer my questions or leave. Go hard or go home!"

Robert was perplexed.

"Stop it, James!" their mother pleaded.

"Robert?" James called him as if he was a small child.

Still perplexed.

"Times up!" James declared, standing up and eyeing Robert. "I'll show you to the door."

Robert looked from James to Mary, who was looking across at Ray. If Ray was aware of what was transpiring around him, he didn't show it as he forked a chunk of meatloaf into his mouth and chewed with his eyes closed. Feeling defeated, Mary dropped her head. Also, feeling defeated, Robert wiped his mouth with his napkin and stood ready to be led to the front door.

"Sit down, Mr. Robert," Ray spoke, slicing into his dressing. He didn't see the relieved look on his mother's and Robert's faces as they stared at him in disbelief. "Unless you *wanna* leave," he added.

Robert looked at James, who had an *'I-wish-you-would'* look on his face.

"Sit down, Robert!" Mary grabbed his arm pulling him back into his chair, but Robert never took his eyes off James.

"Don't mind him," Ray told Robert. "It's two against one."

"So, you're just gonna take this nigga's side?" James asked, looking down at his brother.

"We gotta think about mom on this one," Ray looked up at James. "She knows how we feel about her being involved with dudes. That's why she didn't tell us about him from the jump. She has to care something about him to invite him to Sunday dinner, knowing we would be here."

"Yeah, just like she cared about that last, nigga!" James spat.

"She told me about that," Robert said.

"So, you knew what to expect before you got here," James pointed out.

"I did."

"But you came anyway," James pleaded his case. "Why?"

"For the love of his woman," Ray interjected looking over at his mother, who regarded him with a smile.

"I know you love your mom," Robert said to James. "And I don't have any intentions of hurting her."

"I hope not!" James retorted, taking his seat. To his mother, he said, "I hope you know what you're doing."

"She'll be alright," Ray spoke before she could. "But I have some questions for you, Mr. Robert."

Robert nodded, "Okay."

"You do any kind of drugs?"

"None."

"Drink alcohol?"

"I used to," he replied, making eye contact with Ray. "Until Lynn died."

Ray shot him an inquisitive look.

"Lynn was my wife," Robert explained. "She died in a car accident almost three years ago."

"By the hands of a drunk driver?" Ray wanted to know.

"I was hoping that was the case," he admitted, shaking his head. "But it was the other way around. *She* was the drunk driver. Three other people died in the crash. One was an infant, who'd just been released from the hospital, after being born three days prior.

"I'm sorry to hear that," Ray empathized.

"Yeah, me too," Robert sipped his tea.

Ray asked, "Do you have children?"

"I have a son," Robert answered, smiling at Ray. "His name's Raymond. We also call him, *'Ray'*."

Playa Ray

## CHAPTER 7

Dinner ended up going smooth, everyone came out unscathed. After the chocolate chip pound cake and milk, James and Ray decided to head to the trap and make some money before picking Kim up from work. James called Fred and Black to inform them of their movement. Black vowed that he'd pay a smoker to bring him by later. When they'd arrived on Earnest Street also known as *Rocky Road'*. Ray parked behind Twon's white Buick Regal that was parked behind a black BMW with dark tinted windows. They got out and leaned against the Delta.

"I want one just like that," Ray asserted regarding the BMW. "Same color."

"Just hold that thought," James told him. "Once we get shit on lock, we can all cop one."

At that time, Twon who'd migrated from Iowa seven years ago emerged from the passenger side of the BMW and it pulled off. Twon had lived with his father on Earnest Street until he'd moved in with his girlfriend a few months ago. He was twenty-seven years old, which made him one of the *'big homies'* to James and Ray.

"What up, lil homies," Twon greeted as he approached, giving them dap.

"What it is?" James responded.

"Same shit, different day," Twon answered. "Trying to get it up."

"Who was that in the Beamer?" Ray asked.

"Steve," answered Twon.

"The one with the limousine service?" Ray asked.

"Yeah," Twon answered. "He keeps switching cars on me. I told him about that shit!"

"He might be trying to throw them, folks, off," Ray insisted.

"I've thought about that," Twon replied. "Man, I heard some kids got wet up at the Days Inn last night. Y'all heard about that?"

"Hell, Captain America right here, had a front row seat to the show!" James commented, pointing at Ray.

"How'd you manage that?" Twon asked Ray.

Ray gave him the full run-down.

"Damn!" Twon exclaimed, after quietly taking in the ordeal.

"That's some ugly shit. That shit could've been ugly for you too."

"I told him that shit!" said James. "He's gonna let B.J.'s stupid ass get him knocked off on some bullshit."

"What, you psychic now?" Ray asked, regarding his brother.

"Nah, I ain't no psychic," James answered. "But I can fore-tell bullshit!"

"Y'all know this car, right here?" Twon asked, looking off.

They both shifted their attention in the direction Twon was looking, which was the direction they'd entered Earnest Street. It was already dark, so they couldn't make out the model of the dark-colored car that slowly approached them with the fog lights on and wheels grinding on the loose pebbles that gave Earnest Street its pseudonym.

"I don't know this one," James assured.

The two, distant street lights, didn't help much, but they conceded the car was a Honda as it pulled in behind Ray's car. There were two occupants. The driver killed the engine and lights as the passenger door opened.

"Y'all niggas look like y'all seen a ghost!" Black joked as he approached.

"Yeah, you're a good candidate to star in that new horror movie they're doing," Twon told Black.

"What's the name of the movie, Twon?" James asked, instigating between Twon and Black as always.

"The Creature from the Black Lagoon, Part Two," Twon answered.

That tickled James and Ray.

"I know you didn't!" Black retorted. "Ol' fake Craig Mack looking ass nigga!"

"Nigga, Revlon called," Twon came back. "They wanna know if you'll pose for their new product, '*Dark-N-Ugly*?'"

They cracked on each other until all five of them, including Black's driver listening from the car, was balling in tears. After

Twon got a call from his girlfriend, he dapped the crew and headed home.

"What'd you do in the Cap'?" James asked Black after Twon had left.

"I sold seven sacks," Black told him. "Trap was booming, but them niggas had that shit looking like the fuckin' Olympics, doing hundred-yard dashes to cars 'n shit!"

"I thought the Cap' was always like that," Ray said as he sat up on the hood of his car.

"It is," Black responded. "But niggas were on some more shit! I just said fuck it! Shit, Connie hit me up on my way over here."

"Connie?" James asked.

"From the park yesterday," Black pointed out. "And why y'all ain't got up with her friends yet?"

"How you know we ain't got up with her friends?" asked James.

"Because when I got there, they were asking *'who', 'why', and 'what'* questions," Black answered. "Them hoes wanted some dick."

"You didn't break 'em off?" Ray asked.

"Hell nah! That's y'all job, but I did break Connie off."

"You used protection?" Ray asked with a smirk.

"You know I used protection."

"Nigga, you ain't use no rubber!" James voiced, remembering how Black would periodically blame the founder of contraception for manufacturing a brainchild that hinders a man from enjoying the *'true wetness'* of the pussy.

"And how the fuck you know?" Black challenged.

"Your shit's gonna fuck around and fall off!" James teased. "Then what 'cha gonna do?"

"Buy a strap-on," Ray answered. "Or eat pussy for the rest of his life."

"Y'all ain't talking about shit!" Black countered. "Where the weed at?"

"It's on you this time, ain't it?" asked James.

"I'll do the honors," Black asserted. "Ray let me get a dub."

While they were making the transaction, Shelby a female smoker in her mid-thirties approached. "Hey, y'all!" she greeted with a smile.

"Shelby, I hope you got some money," James said.

Her smile widened. "I always have money."

James caught the hint and automatically ran his eyes over her full-figured body. It was dark, but there was no denying what James saw bulging from the front of her cut-off jean shorts. She wasn't cute, but she was the finest junkie James had ever encountered. Ray admitted the same. Shelby was the first smoker they'd tricked off with when they'd bought their first fifty-dollar slabs of cocaine. They were young and had always shared their fantasies about Shelby, who would always flirt with them when she'd catch them staring at her well-rounded ass.

One night, the big homies all left the trap to attend a birthday bash at Body Tap. Since James and Ray were not old enough to attend, they were the only two left in the trap. It was as if Shelby was waiting on the big homies to leave because as soon as they'd left, she materialized out of nowhere.

They were sitting on the steps of one of the abandoned houses. When she appeared, clad in tight-fitted jeans that flaunted the imprint of her womanhood, and a top that left nothing to the imagination. Being that Shelby was accustomed to exchanging sex for drugs, she didn't beat around the bush when she offered to suck them both off for two dime sacks.

Of course, they agreed, but James had other plans for his share. He had a condom and there was a sofa and table in the abandoned house. On the table were several used candles. James lit the candles while Ray sat on the sofa. Shelby stood in front of them, undid her pants, pulled them off and dropped to her knees to assist Ray with his shorts.

For a moment, James stood there mesmerized by how her dark and juicy ass looked in the candles' light. He was so hard, he had to almost tuck his dick between his legs to get his shorts off. Once that task was complete, he put on the condom and got behind Shelby, who already had Ray's manhood in her mouth. The sound of her slurping and the movement of her body made James grow several more inches.

He was throbbing, with one hand gripping her buttocks, he used his other hand to probe the tip of his penis around until he found the right orifice, almost coming in the process. She let out a short moan as he entered her. He started off at a slow pace, but he was too excited to keep at it.

He had both hands wrapped around her small waist, as he pounded faster and harder. He watched her ass cheeks jerk and vibrate wildly from the constant impact of his mid-section. Then, the condom busted, inviting him to the *'true wetness'* of her womanhood. There was another moan, but this time, it had come from him. He knew he should have pulled out, but it felt like she'd tightened her muscles and wrapped the walls of her vagina around him in a death grip. The thought of impregnating her, or possibly catching an STD, never occurred to him as he tightened his grip around her waist and exploded inside her.

After that night, James would periodically sneak out to rendezvous with her, but their fling ended three months later when Shelby was arrested for cashing and being in possession of stolen checks.

Now James said, "Not tonight, shawty. We're trying to get it up."

"Oh, I can help y'all get it up," she teased.

"What are you trying to do, Shelby?" asked Black.

She eyed him seductively. "I'm trying to get a hit. What are you trying to do?"

"Shit, I'm straight," he told her. "You see dude in that car, right there?"

She looked over at the Honda for a second before turning back to Black. "Yeah."

"That's my nigga, Boston," he told her. "You hook him up, I got you a twenty."

"Aight," she concurred.

Black gave her the product and she climbed into the front passenger seat of the Honda. Seconds later, the car started and rode past them, leaving Earnest Street.

***

Edgewood had been doing numbers ever since Fred arrived earlier that day. Over a year ago, he was considered an '*outsider*,' when he started frequenting these neck of the woods to dally with Michelle. He was already taking a big risk by visiting her in her projects. That was how a lot of dudes became victims of robbery, assault, and even murder. There were times when Fred thought, he'd eventually fall into that category. But, those thoughts subsided on the day Michelle introduced him to Poncho, one of the local dealers in Edgewood.

Poncho, from what Fred perceived, was calling the shots in his hood. He introduced Fred to other dealers and declared to them that Fred had the green light, which signified that he could get money in Edgewood. Shortly after, Fred discovered Poncho's reputation for being a heavyweight, and the one who bedded every bad bitch in the hood. So, it was obvious he and Michelle had something going on, but that was unimportant to Fred. To him, it was just sex, the money he generated in her spot was what kept him at bay.

"You can run the streets with your thugs, I'll be waiting for you," Michelle sang the chorus to *2 Pac's 'Run the Streets'* as she opened the door for, Fred. "You tired? I hope you're hungry."

"Nah, I still haven't digested that fish yet," he reported, rubbing his stomach as he entered.

She locked the door and stood akimbo watching him as he took a seat on the sofa and began counting his money out on the coffee table. She was clad in black spandex shorts and a tank top that beared down on the A-cups of her petite frame.

"Are you tired?" She asked again, moving closer to the table.

"Not really," he answered, not looking up. He knew what she was getting at, but he still asked, "Why?"

"Cause, I need some."

## CHAPTER 8

It had been almost thirty minutes since Shelby left with Boston, but the crew had not taken much notice, once they started reminiscing about the past. James had occasionally checked his watch, now he saw it was almost eleven. Kim would be getting off soon but wouldn't be ready until around eleven-thirty. So, they had enough time.

"Ray, you gotta take me to get a rental car tomorrow," James said, exhaling weed smoke.

"That's a bet," Ray agreed. "What time?"

"Whenever you get up and get situated," James told him. "You don't have plans, do you?"

"Who is this, right here?" Black inquired, looking towards the top of Earnest Street, at an approaching car.

They were all looking in that direction, but the headlights made it difficult to decipher the make and model. Once it pulled to a stop in front of them, they saw that it was a white Dodge Intrepid, occupied by three white men.

"You guys know where we can cop some blow?" the driver inquired.

"Fuck no!" James retorted. "Better take y'all asses back to Cabbage Town!"

"We'll pay you for your troubles," promised the guy in the rear seat.

"Y'all in the wrong hood pimp," Ray spoke easing down off the hood of his car. "This is a drug-free zone."

The men began conversing amidst each other in low tones. In the course of the conversation, the driver shifted the gear into park.

"Man, this shit don't look, right," Black stated.

"Nah, it don't," Ray agreed. "This might be—"

Before he could complete the sentence, the men lunged from the car shouting, "Freeze police!"

\*\*\*

53

Kim had just pulled the last of the trash in the dining area and was tying the trash bag, when her friend, Patrice approached.

"You aight, girl?" she asked.

"Yeah, I'm cool," Kim answered. "Just tired as hell."

"I know, John said I can go ahead and leave since my mom is already out there," Patrice told her. "My uncle should have my car fixed tomorrow."

"Hell, we don't work tomorrow," Kim reminded her.

"I know, but that don't mean you can't go with me to get my hair fixed." She tugged on Kim's brown micro-braids. "You got yours fixed."

"My stylist makes house calls," Kim told her. "If you want, I'll call her tonight and make you an appointment. She'll do it at my house."

"That's too risky."

"What'd you mean?"

"I can't let my baby see me like this!"

"Girl, I know, you ain't talking about Ray?"

"Who else would I be talking about?"

Kim couldn't help but laugh. "Girl, you're crazy!"

"I just wanna sit on those sexy-ass lips of his!" she admitted. "Tell me that nigga don't have no sexy, pussy-pleasing lips!"

"I don't look at Ray like that!" Kim protested with a disgusted look on her face.

"That's good!" Patrice pointed an accusing finger at Kim. "Cause, we'll go toe-to-toe 'bout that one but go ahead and make the appointment."

"I'll do that," Kim promised. "Just get some rest cause she may schedule you for in the morning."

"Okay, good night, baby."

"Goodnight."

They hugged, then Patrice made her exit. Kim checked the time on her cell phone, 11:05 pm.

\*\*\*

Black felt like he'd run a hundred-yard dash as he collapsed behind some bushes and peered out to see if any of the pursuers were still on his trail. He didn't see anyone, he'd figured the trio in the Dodge were undercovers. Before the cops could get both legs out the car, the crew bolted between two abandoned houses, where there were absolutely no light and the setting was something similar to a miniature forest, being that the land had not been tended to in centuries. Then James insisted they split up.

Black didn't know every pathway in Bland Town like Ray and James, but as soon as his eyes adjusted to the dark, he was tracking through the vast meadow, dodging trees and hopping over old discarded appliances like a cadet in Basic Combat Training. However, the faint sounds of footsteps and a radio transmitter let him know someone was on his tail. Therefore, without looking back, he accelerated and fleetingly hiked over rows of railroad tracks until he came to the back of a warehouse building that was turned into an art gallery.

In one swift motion, Black hoisted himself over the fence leading to the well-lit parking lot. From there, he could see the main road, which was Marietta Boulevard. His plan was to casually cross the lot – careful not to raise suspicion from the two security guards occupying the booth at the entrance to the main street and make that ten-minute walk to Knight Park, and see if he could score a ride back to Capital Homes.

What he saw on Marietta Boulevard, made him stop in his tracks, and his heart dropped to his stomach. Police cars – marked and unmarked – lagged and circled around like they were looking for someone—*him*! Now, behind the bushes, and lying on his back, Black finally reined hold of his breathing as he replayed the scenes of the day over in his mind. He couldn't help but think about how Nikki begged him to stay home with her and the kids. When he declined, she then implored him to leave his gun at home.

Obviously, she felt something was going to happen. Whenever she'd feel like that, she was usually right. He disregarded her first request, but to mitigate her worries, he granted her second request by leaving his gun. He snapped out of his thoughts when a pair of headlights flashed through his nature-made fortress. He didn't hear the vehicle approach, due to the rumbling of the boxcars on a passing train. The noise gradually became distant, indicating the last of the railroad cars had passed.

Now, there was a new sound that bugged him because the sound seemed close. It sounded like the engine of some kind of vehicle sitting in one spot. Black turned over on the damp land, positioning himself on his stomach, and peered through the hedges. His guessing was exact: there was a vehicle parked right in front of the bushes. A white Ford Bronco, but this wasn't any ordinary truck. This truck was equipped with chrome front-to-rear guardrails, blue strobe lights, and a logo plastered on the passenger door that read, 'K-9 UNIT.'

As if things couldn't get any worse, at that very moment, he realized that he'd forgotten to put his cell phone on vibrate, because it came alive, sounding like it was hooked up to an amplifier. Apprehension flooded Black as he nervously snatched the phone from his pocket and extracted the battery. Silence, but apparently, the officer had heard it because he swung the driver's door open and dismounted. Black found himself looking under the truck at the driver's boots as he walked towards the rear of the truck. The next sound was unmistakable: the officer opened the cargo area of the Bronco.

\*\*\*

Ray didn't have a definite plan as he ran along the single railroad track that ran into a range of tracks in a fork-in-the-road pattern, but he was far from the conjunction as his legs got heavier, chest got tighter, and lungs felt as if they were going to collapse at any moment. His running converted into a strenuous jog and with every step, he silently cursed the fact that he had not outgrown his asthma.

Feeling like he couldn't go any further, Ray stopped, almost falling face down to the earth when his knees nearly buckled, but he held fast, leaning forward, resting his hands on his knees, holding them like he didn't trust them to function properly on their own. Holding his position, he glanced over his shoulder to see if anyone had followed his trail. It was clear, the only movement of the tracks was a train that was approaching to the left of him. He could see the effulgent lights of the Brobdingnagian locomotive through the thick array of trees that separated the fork. Then, something else caught his attention. It was the high beam of a lamp bulb shining down on him from the bridge on Huff Road. The light wasn't blinding, considering the distance. Therefore, he could distinguish the vehicle it protruded from—*a cop's car*! He'd been spotted!

"Stand where you are!" A disembodied male's voice boomed through the bullhorn of the car.

"Yeah, right," Ray mumbled as he coerced his legs to continue towards the conjunction.

There was a case of wooden stairs leading up to Marietta Boulevard, but the train was the only thing that segregated him from the stairs – not to mention Knight Park, which was just across the street. Ray's knees almost gave out on him again as he reached the train and stopped. He could see the stairs through the gaps of the passing cars but couldn't see where the cars ended. Holding his knees again, and trying to restrain his breathing, Ray took another glance at the stairs through the gaps of the passing boxcars and noticed a squad car come to a stop at the top of them.

Two male officers dismounted and stood in front of the car. The area was dimly lit by lamp posts, so Ray was certain they could see him. This left him with two choices: one, stand there and wait to be arrested, or two catch the train. He reminded himself that he hadn't discarded his gun, or his drugs because he had shaken his pursuers, less than a minute into the chase. Therefore, he was still dirty, he'd never had a possession charge and didn't plan on catching one tonight.

Looking to his left, he could now see the rear of the train approaching. Breaking into a run, he trotted alongside the train that seemed to be going at least twenty miles per hour as railcars passed him. Slipping and sliding on the confetti-like granite that inlaid the tracks to maintain his footing, he reached up and took hold of the steel ladder of a passing car, allowing himself to be snatched off his feet like a rag doll.

In a pull-up motion, Ray pulled his legs up, planting his feet at the bottom of the ladder. This was something he'd performed well when he and other kids used to play on the trains. It was fun but dangerous. He'd seen a lot of peers fall off, but never under the trains. Now, Ray was nearing the bridge that segmented Bland Town and Knight Park. He looked back but couldn't tell what the officers were doing. As he looked towards the bridge, he saw a helicopter circling the railroad's shipping yard up ahead with the high beam and was now coming his way. He quickly climbed between the cars to the other side as the lambent light swept over him.

Apparently, they didn't see him because the aircraft kept going. Ray was relieved, he was also relieved that the train was taking the left curve and not going straight ahead, which led to the shipping yard. The curve meant the train was going to travel through Maddox Park—*his destination*!

***

If the officer planned to let the dog out on Black, he would never know, because as soon as a call came over the radio about a suspect running east on the railroad tracks and coming upon Northside Drive, the officer slammed the cargo door shut and sped out of there. Black had been holding his breath through the whole ordeal. Now, he lay motionless behind the bushes, on his back, taking in the sounds of people leaving the building, talking, laughing, starting their vehicles and…the drone of a helicopter—*a helicopter*?

Quickly, Black got to his knees and peered over the top of the hedges. The aircraft was about a hundred yards out, shinning its ominous searchlight from the tracks to the warehouses that lined this side of the street. Surveying the parking lot, Black spotted a white Chevy Suburban. The crowd was getting thicker, and the helicopter was getting closer. Without giving it any more thought, Black, got to his feet and nonchalantly walked towards the truck.

There was no way he could blend in – being that this was an all-white and casually dressed crowd, but lucky for him, the people had stopped to take interest in the *'air show.'* That was his chance to make his move. He quickly got down and scooted up under the truck, with his head closer to the motor. He could feel the spilled oil soak through his shirt and stick to his back. From the sounds of the helicopter, Black could tell that it was in the vicinity. The lamp swept the parking lot once, twice, then hovered over the truck, as if it was equipped with X-ray.

Was it? Obviously not, because the helicopter moved on. Then, Black heard the faint click of the truck's locks, and the clicking of two pairs of heels as they neared the truck.

"I wonder what they're looking for," one of the women asserted.

"Probably a serial killer," the other assumed.

The women climbed into the truck, and the engine came to life. Black didn't know if the driver intended to immediately pull off, but he knew, he couldn't stay under there a second longer. Sliding from under the truck, he sat up and toyed with his laces as if tying his shoes.

"Are you a serial killer?" The female's voice – not to mention the question took Black by surprise. He looked up to see that the passenger window was rolled down, and the two women were smiling down at him, anticipating his answer.

"Nah," Black answered, feeling strange. "I'm a drug dealer."

Hearing his answer, the women conferred with each other for a few seconds. Then the passenger asked, "Do you need a ride?"

\*\*\*

"Why the fuck is he not answering the phone?" Kim asked as she pressed 'end' on her cell phone and looked out to see if anyone had pulled into the parking lot.

She'd called James twice and acquired his voicemail both times. Perhaps he was getting his dick sucked by that tramp Brenda, she thought. Maybe she should call Ray. If he didn't answer, then he was getting his dick sucked, too—*by Brenda*! Kim dialed Ray's number and listened to his ringtone, which was *Organization's 'Can't Stop No Playa.'*

\*\*\*

James tossed his drugs and gun as he fled, purposefully staying in the middle of the track. His pursuers – all three of them were literally 'falling behind.' He could hear them swear out loud every time one of them stumbled or fell. The railroad tracks had always served as a means of escape when running from the law because obviously, they were used to running track. Not railroad tracks.

At the rate that James' pursuers were going, they couldn't catch a turtle on these tracks. They were so far behind, he felt he could stop and answer his cell phone vibrating in his hand, but all he could do was look at the lit screen to see who was calling.

Kim! He'd forgotten that he and Ray had to pick her up from work. The phone vibrated again. He thought about answering it, and through breaths explaining to her what was taking place, but the droning sounds of a helicopter concluded that thought. James looked back and conceded that his luck had just run out. The helicopter was about a hundred yards out and closing.

Seeing that he was about twenty-five yards away from the bridge above Northside Drive, he accelerated. As he reached the bridge, he thrust the phone into his pocket and proceeded to climb down. All he had to do was make it to Krystal's. There, he would eat and chill until everything died down. He would also call Kim and fill her in on tonight's fiasco. James was off the bridge, but as soon as his feet touched solid ground, two patrol cars with lights flashing and sirens blaring, came from opposite directions, and simultaneously skidded to a halt in front of him, but James wasn't hearing this.

He broke into a run in the direction of Krystal's. More cars showed up. The K-9 Unit showed up. The high beam that shined down on him indicated the helicopter had finally showed up. Knowing the law, James knew they could only charge him with eluding authority, and probably possession of marijuana, less than an ounce, for the piece of blunt he had in his pocket.

Getting to the intersection, James stopped, pulled his blunt and lighter from his pocket and blazed up as the squad cars surrounded him. Slipping the lighter back into his pocket, he sat on the ground with his knees bent, and the intent to finish his blunt. The helicopter's beam lingered on him. Officers were out of their vehicles with their weapons drawn, but no one commanded him to freeze or to put his hands where they could see them because he was as 'frozen' as he was going to get, and his hands…well, they could vividly see what his hands were doing.

*'This shit like a scene from a movie,'* James thought as he took another pull on his blunt and gandered across the street at Krystal's. The thought of a double bacon and cheese from Krystal's watered his dry mouth.

***

The boxcar that Ray was clinging to had approached the bridge over Bankhead Highway and now entered Maddox Park. Now he had to pull another dangerous maneuver to get off the train that had gradually increased its speed, but a train's speed had never been a problem to him. He moved his hands two bars down and in a reverse pull-up motion, lowered himself to the ground with his body turned slightly forward. Once his feet found the gravel, he pedaled, half-running, half-gliding alongside the train as he still held on to the bar. Once he'd let go, it took every effort he could muster not to lose his footing and fall forward.

After about twelve yards, Ray gained control of his legs. Tired, he sat on the yellow guardrail and watched the last of the railcars go by. He wanted to cross over to the picnic tables under the shed and lie on one, but he noticed a female already occupying one, lying on her back, and she wasn't alone. There was a man standing between her legs with his pants to his knees – and her skirt up – giving her the business. His moaning was inaudible, but Ray could faintly hear her pleas of *'go deeper'* and *'fuck me harder!'*

The man must have felt the heat from Ray's eyeballs because he opened his eyes and looked directly at Ray. The man's reaction alerted his partner, who had to tilt her head upward to see Ray, she smiled. Feeling like he'd invaded these people's privacy, Ray swung his legs over the rail, turning his back to them. That's when he remembered that his cell phone had vibrated while he was 'joyriding' on the train. He pulled the phone from his pocket and checked the caller I.D. Seeing Kim's number, he pressed *Send*.

"Why haven't y'all picked me up yet?" Kim demanded answering. "And what bitch got James so fucked up he can't answer his damn phone?"

"He's not answering his phone?' Ray asked, now concerned.

"Nah, that nigga ain't answering. Ain't he with you?"

"No," Ray answered, then gave her the full scoop on what induced the separation.

"So, you don't know if he got caught?"

"I doubt it. Can you find a ride home?"

"I can ask my manager."

"Do that and let me know what's up. I gotta contemplate my next move."

Ray hung up and tried James number. The voicemail came on. He hung up without leaving a message. If James had been arrested, Ray hoped like hell he didn't get caught with the drugs and gun—especially the gun! Ray knew Fred was stationed in Edgewood with Michelle, and possibly getting to the money. He also knew Fred would drop everything for his boys if they needed him, and vice versa.

For some reason, Ray felt it would be selfish of him to disturb his friend, because he didn't have a ride when the Bankhead Train Station was just across the street from the park, and for some reason, he did not feel right about going home tonight, but where would he go? Who would he call to come pick him up?

B.J.! He'd forgotten he'd promised to call B.J. after the re-up. He couldn't believe he'd forgotten something that was almost routine. Yes, he would call B.J. to pick him up and take him to a hotel. Then, tomorrow he would check for James and Black. While he was scanning his phone for B.J.'s number, it vibrated, startling him, almost causing him to drop it. The name and number on the screen were very unfamiliar.

"Yeah?" he answered.

"You don't keep your promises, do you?" the familiar female's voice accused.

*'Sylvia!'* he thought instantly. "I was just telling myself that," Ray told her. "So, do you want my apology or my excuse.

"Both," she snapped. "Then you have to make it up to me."

"And how would I do that?"

"I'll tell you when you get here."

"What!"

"You heard me!" Sylvia replied. "You can't make it up to me over the phone."

*'This girl is impossible,'* he thought, but couldn't deny how much he loved a woman who took charge.

"Barbecue or mildew!" she prompted.

"Shawty, I'm stranded," he admitted.

"Bullshit!"

"I'm serious."

She was quiet. All Ray could hear in the background was a radio, playing Toni Braxton's *'Just Be a Man About it.'*

"Where are you?" she finally asked.

"Same place I met you."

"At the park?" she sounded incredulous.

"Yeah."

"And how'd you manage to get stranded up the street from me?" she asked. "You know I stay in Overlook Atlanta, right?"

"Yeah."

"You know what?" she caught an attitude. "I should've known you were gonna play these childish-ass games! I don't even know why the fuck—"

"I'll be standing in the same spot we met. You want me, you got ten minutes to show up, or I'm catching the train!" he cut her off, then ended the call before she could respond. He looked across the street at the train station and hoped like hell she'd show. Maybe he should've asked if she had a car.

# CHAPTER 9

"See, I told you they would fit," Sylvia stated when Ray reentered her bedroom, clad in a pair of her boxer shorts and a t-shirt.

She'd picked him up in her aunt's Toyota Camry. When he asked her to take him to a hotel, she insisted he spend the night with her, stating that her room was free, and came with complimentary, unlimited sex. Ray could not resist that!

He didn't meet her aunt, because she was in her bedroom with the door closed. So, he relished a thirty-minute shower and made it back to Sylvia's room, where she was curled up on the bed watching T.V., clad in a pair of boxer shorts and a tank-top. Ray walked over to the dresser and opened the top drawer, lifting some of her boxers and panties, he saw that his money and gun were still there.

"I'm not gonna steal from you," she stated, getting off the bed, locking the door.

Ray noted how her ass stretched the cloth of her boxers looking almost like spandex. He had to look away to keep from getting aroused.

"I can't see myself using body spray," he said, regarding her panoply of cosmetics, hoping to deflect his lustful thoughts. "I hope you got some real stuff."

"Of course, I got some real stuff," she said as she sauntered up to him and began pulling the t-shirt over his head. Once the shirt was off, she gently pushed him down on the bed and mounted him.

Ray could no longer contain his erection. After all, it had been over two weeks. Sylvia reached over and extinguished the lamp on the nightstand, leaving them illuminated by the glow of the T.V. Then, she brought her mouth down on his, inserting her tongue. Naturally, Ray wouldn't play the 'kissing game' with a female he didn't know much about, but this time, he made an exception. As he kissed her back, he placed his hands on her waist at the elastic of her boxers.

He could not help it! Ray wormed his fingers under the elastic and extended his arms until his hands came in contact with her ex-tremely-soft ass, gripping both cheeks.

"You wouldn't know what to do with all that," she whispered into his ear.

"Oh yeah?"

"Yeah."

She pinned his hands to the bed and started kissing him on the neck. Then she made her way down to his chest and took one of his nipples into her mouth, sucking and licking it in a circular motion. It felt good to him, but it was taking entirely too long. Foreplay – Ray felt – was a tactic used to stimulate a person. He was beyond stimulation! Unable to stand another second of this, Ray grabbed her waist and rolled over, planting her on the bed, while he was on top of her.

"Oh, you're one of those straight-to-action men, huh?" she asked, with a seductive smile on her face.

"Pretty much."

***

James could not believe he'd gotten caught. Most of all, he could not believe that his initial pursuer had found the drugs and gun. There was no way they were supposed to have found those items. He knew he was well out of their sights when he'd discarded them and for the umpteenth time, he wondered why all three officers pursued him in lieu of branching off. He felt like he was their primary target.

James thought about assuming an alias, but once they'd brought the gun and drugs in a Ziploc and showed it to him while he was handcuffed in the back seat of a squad car, he knew he wouldn't be able to get a bond and post it before his fingerprints came back.

"Mr. Young, I'm going to deny your attorney's request for bond and I'm going to bound the case over to the Superior Court of Fulton County," the white-haired male judge declared. "You will remain at the Pretrial Detention Center until you're transferred to the Fulton County Jail. Next case!"

James was shackled and cuffed to the front, he ignored his two-minute Public Defender's hand, and allowed an officer to escort him out of the courtroom, back to the musty-smelling holding cell where he and about thirty other men had been held up for the past four hours or so.

The officer took the restraints off before letting James back into the cell. Before entering, he pulled his shirt up to his nose, seeing that everyone who was awake, had their noses covered, indicating someone had 'let one go' again. It was bad enough that, there were no windows and the air vents were there for decoration because neither one did a thing for the urine and foul body odor that permeated the small cell.

There was one metal sink and toilet that sat in plain view, so if anyone had to take a shit, not only could a portion of the cell see them, but the smell would linger in the air forever. Therefore, they would have to adhere to the respectable code: drop and flush. There was no room on the steel bench, so after stepping over sleeping bodies, James found a place on the wall, placed his back on it, and was careful not to bump into the guy, on the phone crying to mother like he'd been doing for hours.

James looked at his watch, it was 9:29 am, and he still had not picked up the phone to inform anyone of his whereabouts. The only person he could call collect was his grandmother in Decatur, but he had no plans of calling her to tell her that her grandson was back in jail. Somehow, he wished he could avoid this routine call to save her the heartache, but the call had to be made. He had to check on Kim and let Ray know his name was cleared, so it was okay to pick up his car from the impound. When the cops questioned him about the car, James told them his brother let him borrow it. When they asked about the keys, he claimed to have lost them in the chase. When they'd asked about the other two 'perpetrators,' that's when James exercised his right to remain silent.

When he yawned, it reminded him that he had not closed his eyes for no more than three seconds since his arrest. He could never see himself curled up on the floor of a holding cell, asleep, but once they classified him to a cell, it was a done deal!

\*\*\*

"Does anybody live around here?" Connie asked Ray as she slowly drove her Ford Focus over the pebbles of Earnest Street.

Sylvia's aunt left that morning for work, so Sylvia, after washing Ray's clothes at the laundromat, called Connie to take Ray home, but Ray had other affairs to tend to before going home. Connie protested at first, but Ray offered to fill up the gas tank and buy everyone, including Meeka, who was seated in the front passenger seat, lunch. While he and Sylvia waited on their ride, Sylvia cooked breakfast and he made a few phone calls. He called Kim and had her call Pretrial on three-way, to find out if James had been arrested.

It was confirmed that James was arrested and charged with eluding authority, possession of cocaine and possession of a firearm. Ray had a hard time believing James had got caught with these things on him. The fact that James didn't use an alias, also shocked him.

After hanging up with Kim, Ray phoned Black, only to have Nikki answer and tell him Black was asleep. Then, he called Fred and gave him the scoop. They vowed to meet up, later.

"A few people," Ray now answered Connie's question. "We can ride out, they got the car."

"You don't know what impound they took it to?" Sylvia, who was seated beside him asked.

Ray looked over at her. She wouldn't win a beauty pageant, but the girl had a salient sex appeal about her. He loved the way her mouth was set, the way her bottom lip protruded a little farther than the top. That was the same mouth that had awakened him from his sleep this morning. Now he'd heard a lot of guys boast about awakening to a female sucking them off, but he'd never experienced it, until this morning.

"Not yet," he answered.

\*\*\*

"Ray called you," Nikki told Black when he'd come out of the bedroom.

She was curled up on the sofa, eating potato chips and watching T.V.

"What'd he say?"

"To let you know he called."

"James ain't hit?"

"Did I say James hit?" she caught an attitude.

Black scowled at her, but she disregarded the look by gluing her eyes back to the TV, with her lips poked out. That signified she was mad about something, but right now, he didn't feel up to finding out. To do so meant he would have to engage in one of her frivolous and childish arguments.

*'Not right now,'* he thought as he entered the bathroom, feeling like he hadn't pissed in centuries.

As he stood over the toilet, draining his bladder, he reverted his thoughts to the White women he'd hitched a ride with last night. He couldn't remember their names, but he remembered them being best friends, unhappily married with children and residing in Gwinnett County. Most importantly he remembered that they were so anxious to know why there was a 'worldwide manhunt' for a mere drug dealer.

Black, who was grateful for the ride that may have saved him a trip to jail, felt much obliged to tell them the story. From when the undercover officers pulled up, to the moment they'd offered him a lift, but that wasn't enough. They wanted to hear about the 'hood,' and what it was like for him growing up in such a place. So, feeling comfortable with his small audience, Black told his story, including Fred, James, and Ray. The girls listened attentively. The passenger shed her seatbelt and turned around, facing him, with her legs curled up under her.

As they rode on Northside Drive, they came upon the traffic light that ran across University Avenue. The light was red, Black looked over at the Burger King that Kim works at, and wondered if she'd already gone home, seeing that there were still employees inside.

"How big is your dick?" the driver asked, smiling back at Black, who was seated behind her friend.

Stunned by the whimsical question, Black looked over at the passenger and realized he was the only one shocked by it because her expression was parallel to the drivers. Perhaps they were accustomed to playing this game with strangers.

"I don't know," he answered, feeling constrained, but readying himself for whatever ensued.

"You don't know how big your dick is?" Asked the passenger, looking down as if she could see through the fabric of his shorts.

"Hell no!" he answered. "I mean, I don't just—"

"Let us see it!" The driver cut him off and switched the gear into park, activating the interior lights.

"Yeah, let us see it!" her friend chimed.

Black could not believe what he was hearing. He would have blamed it on the weed, had his high not dissipated the second the officers bolted from their car with the intent of an arrest.

"You're not shy, are you?" the passenger teased.

"Maybe he's afraid we're gonna cut it off and take it home with us," the driver pitched in.

"Yeah, maybe I can sew it on to Ben."

"Who the fuck is Ben?" Black inquired, not liking the fact that his dick had become the main topic of the evening.

"Ben is my poodle," the passenger explained. "He's always hunching on people's legs with that little pink thing coming out."

"Yeah, that horny-ass mutt could smell pussy through a bullet-proof glass!" said the driver. "It's bad when you attract more attention from a dog than you do from your own husband."

"He turns you on, too?" her friend asked her.

"Girl, if Ben catches me one night when I'm pissy drunk, he just might get lucky!" she declared, and both of them erupted with laughter, slapping palms.

"Man, y'all trippin'," Black asserted, looking over again at the Burger King's parking lot as a dark-colored Buick Lesabre pulled in. Seconds later, a female employee emerged from the building, headed for the car. She looked like Kim, but Black knew better than to think Kim would step out on James like that.

"We're sorry, we just got a little carried away," the driver apologized, diverting Black's attention. "So, are you going to let us see, or do we have to sit here, all night?"

"Trust me—" the passenger said, "—we're in no hurry to get home to our bratty kids and boring husbands."

"It doesn't have to be hard," said the driver. "We just wanna see it."

Truth be told, he was nowhere near hard. This had never happened before. Maybe they'd frightened his 'little man' with their bold antic but being the 'ladies' man he was, he gave in. Seeing that the light was already green, he hastily undid his belt, while they watched with voracity. Ready to get it over with, Black pulled his shorts and boxers down past his knees, revealing his flaccid manhood that rested on his thigh.

"Wow!" they both marveled in unison.

The driver asked, "Can we touch it?"

"Yeah, let us touch it!" the passenger agreed.

Before Black could muster a quarter of an answer, they were hanging over their seats, touching, feeling and stroking his penis and testicles with eagerness. That was sufficient enough to make little man stand up.

"It's alive!" the passenger exclaimed, holding it in a firm grip, just above her friend's grip. "Anal sex would definitely be out of the question for you!"

The sound of the car's horn, startled them, causing them to withdraw to their positions. Black fought to get his shorts up over his erection as the driver extinguished the interior lights and drove on. Not wanting to let them know where he lived, he asked to be dropped off downtown, and walked the rest of the way, thinking of them, hoping to run into them again, whatever their names were.

"Why'd you let me sleep so late?" Black asked Nikki when he re-entered the living room.

"Nobody told you to stay out all night, hoe-hopping," she retorted, not taking her eyes off the set.

"How the hell you figure I was out hoe-hopping?"

"Cause you didn't tell me you were leaving out the hood last night."

"Is that why you think—"

"Yep!"

"Thank God you're not a detective!" he asserted. "The whole world would be in prison fuckin' with your non-investigating ass!"

"Whatever!"

"I can't get a hug?"

"Nope!"

"Man, why you sitting over there flexing?" he asked, smiling knowing if he started kissing on her neck, she would be begging him to fuck her, right there on the couch. "So, you mad at me?"

"Yep!"

"Well, you can stay mad, ol' nappy-head heifer!" he asserted smiling, heading for the kids' room.

"Black-ass tar baby!" she shot back, suppressing a smile.

Black heard her but didn't look back as he entered his children's room, approaching the crib, where his eight-month-old son slept. Lil' Keith would normally be awake by now. Perhaps the cool air from the air conditioner wedged in the living room window, kept him sedated. Nicole had spent the weekend at Nikki's parents' home, in Florida, and was expected back today. It would be her first time going to Disney World and he wasn't the one to accompany her.

While he was in his thoughts, Nikki crept up behind him, wrapping her arms around his waist and resting her head on his back. He vowed to not let his children grow up in the projects, but if this lick didn't work—

## CHAPTER 10

"Cellmate?"

James rolled over out of his sleep, on the top bunk and looked into the face of a guy who may have been an older version of Harry Potter. This was strange to him because he didn't remember anyone being in the cell when he arrived. Although when he arrived, he tossed his hygiene kit in the corner and climbed into his bunk without taking anything off.

"Supper," Harry Potter announced.

James looked over at the desk, where two trays sat, one on top of the other. It looked like spaghetti, but just the thought of reverting to this slop again made him queasy. Therefore, he just rolled back over to resume his slumber.

"You're not eating?" asked Harry Potter.

"You can have it."

"Gee, thanks!" was the last thing he heard from Harry Potter as he drifted back into la-la land.

When he awoke again, the room was dark. It was also dark outside. He leaned over the bunk to see if Harry Potter was asleep. Harry Potter was not there. Then, he noticed the cell door was ajar. That signified it was free time. At this time, detainees were watching television, using the phones, taking showers, playing basketball, or telling lies. Remembering that he had to use the phone, he lunged out of his rack and fumbled with his hygiene kit for his toothbrush and toothpaste.

After handling his hygiene, he emerged from the cell, surveying his housing unit. A control panel sat in the center of the dorm, where a Black female officer was stationed. Being that Pretrial only issued uniforms to detainees with high profile cases such as murder, rape, armed robbery and so on – as well as trustees, everyone else still had on their street attire.

James' cell was downstairs, so he didn't have to do much traveling to obtain one of the phones mounted to a line of pillars, but right now, they were all occupied. Harry Potter was on a phone directly in front of the cell. Harry Potter looked like a poster child for a Feed the Homeless ad, clad in a black t-shirt with a Georgia Bull-dogs' logo on the front and back, brown cut-off dress pants, and brown Penny Loafers with no socks.

"You're awake!" Harry Potter exclaimed, now noticing him.

"Yeah, I guess I am," James responded. "Who got that phone after you?"

"You do, but free-time is almost up."

James looked at his watch. It was 9:07 p.m. He didn't know the exact time free-time started or ended, but he knew he would have to remit his call until tomorrow.

"I could have my wife call your family on three-way if you need to let them know where you are," Harry Potter offered.

From the looks of things, James didn't really have much of a choice. He really needed to let Ray know there wasn't a warrant out for his arrest for his car being at the scene. He knew Ray had to be worried about that. Besides, this call would save their grandmother the heartache.

"Yeah, I need to."

\*\*\*

"I guess he's not gonna call," Ray asserted, looking at his watch.

They had all vowed to meet up at Fred's place. After the girls dropped him off at home, Ray immediately called B.J. to come pick him up. They arrived in Knight Park, shortly after five o'clock. Black who'd paid Boston to chauffeur him, was already present. They'd been awaiting James' call, so they would know what procedures they had to conduct to get him out.

Now they were standing in front of Fred's house, on the road that also acted as a driveway for the line of houses that went to the end of Niles Avenue.

"That's what it looks like," Fred replied. "What y'all bout to get into?"

"Shit! I'm 'bout to head to the crib," Black answered. 'Lil Keith got a doctor's appointment in the morning."

"I still don't trust my crib," said Ray. "So, I'ma cop me a room somewhere."

"Nigga, you can crash here," Fred told him. "Unless you're still scared of rats."

"Shit, those ain't rats y'all got," Ray responded. "They're niggas!"

"No, not niggas!" Black laughed.

"Hell yeah!" Ray fed into it. "Them niggas be all in a nigga's pockets while a nigga sleep! Trying on a nigga's shoes 'n shit!"

Fred had to join in on the laughter because he'd set himself up for that one. He'd forgotten that Ray had been crowned 'Class Clown of the Year'— every year!

"You got down, ol' ugly-ass nigga!" Fred admitted, giving him dap.

"No doubt," Ray accepted the compliment. "But I'ma still cop me a room for a few days."

"Well let me know where you at," Fred told him. "And hit me up as soon as you hear from James."

"You know I'ma do that."

They all dapped and vowed to get up with each other later. Then, Ray and B.J. climbed into B.J.'s '97 Chevy Impala and rode off.

"Budget Inn?" asked B.J.

"Yeah," Ray answered. "Crank that Troy back up."

B.J. turned on the radio, and *Pastor Troy's Made* came roaring through the customized sound system as they neared Marietta Boulevard. As soon as they turned on Marietta, Ray's phone vibrated in his lap. The name and number on the screen were new. He silenced the radio before answering it.

"Yeah?"

"Ray?" James' voice came through the phone.

"Who else would be answering my phone?" Ray replied. "And what the hell you—"

"Ray, I don't have much time to talk," James cut in. "So, you gotta listen."

"A'ight."

"I told them, folks, you let me borrow the car, so they're not looking for you. I went to my hearing this morning. They denied bond and bounded me over to Fulton. I'll hit you and Kim up when I get there and let y'all know what the visitation days are. Until then, just—"

"Free-time is now over! Free-time is now over!" Ray heard a female's voice announce over the P.A. system.

"Ray?"

"I'm here."

"Just chill and keep an eye on my wife."

"A'ight."

"Tell the crew I'll get at them when I hit Rice Street."

"That's what's up."

"One!"

"One!" Ray concluded the call.

"What's the word?" asked B.J.

"Take me home."

***

"I've heard of it," James said. "But I thought it was some kind of sexual stimulation drug."

James and Harry Potter – whose real name was Milton- had been chatting since the conclusion of free-time. James had discovered that Milton was married with three children and that he and his brother owned a small club in Buckhead. He was arrested for a DUI and minor traffic violations.

"Heck no!" Milton replied. He was sitting Indian-style on his bunk, while James sat on the desk, with his feet in the chair. "I think Ecstasy is about to be the next best thing. It's a wonder drug and it's gradually becoming prevalent in Georgia. By the summer of two thousand three, it should be flooding the streets."

"A wonder drug, huh?"

"Dude you should see people's reactions when they're on it. It's amazing!"

76

"What if I wanted to get my hands on some? How do I go about it?" James asked.

"That would be kinda hard, right now," Milton answered. "First, you'll have to find a supplier. These guys are secretly operating in small places."

"Like clubs," James concluded, nodding.

"Yeah."

"So, there's a supplier at your club."

"Barely."

"*Barely?*" James repeated.

"This guy comes in with like ten to twenty pills whenever he shows up."

"And how often is that?"

"Every other week."

"You know him?"

"I just met him, but my brother knows him."

"Your brother may have his hands on a supply."

"I doubt it."

"You don't think—"

"James Young!" a male's voice came over the small intercom mounted to the wall, cutting him off.

"What's up?" James answered.

"Pack it up!" the disembodied voice told him. "You're shipping out to Fulton County."

"A'ight."

Milton said, "I hear it's pretty rough over there."

"It's what you make it," James told him.

Playa Ray

## CHAPTER 11

The next day, Ray awoke around 9:30 a.m. feeling exuberant not to mention, sexually aroused. For some reason, he could not stop thinking about Sylvia. He went to sleep thinking about Sylvia. He dreamed about Sylvia. He woke up thinking about Sylvia. Sylvia-Sylvia-Sylvia!

After showering and consuming a half box of Honey Combs, Ray got the phone book, his fully-charged cell phone, and went to work at the kitchen table. He had to find out which impound was holding his baby hostage. Plus, he had to hurry, because it was 11:33 and he'd told Sylvia to have Connie there by twelve. It had taken only three calls for him to find out his car was at the City's impound downtown, and ready to be picked up.

***

"Yes, how may I help you?" the blonde behind the desk, asked.

"I called earlier about my car that was impounded Sunday," Ray told her.

"Name?" she asked, typing on her keypad.

"Ray Young."

"Make and model of your vehicle?"

He told her.

"Color?"

"Black."

"One moment." She grabbed her phone's receiver.

Ray turned his back to her and was now facing Sylvia and Connie, who were sitting side-by-side in the lobby, bickering over the contents of some magazine they pursued together. He wondered if Sylvia knew that the slightest movement of her legs revealed the lime colored thong she wore under her matching mini skirt. She had to know, he thought. Perhaps she didn't care. She must have felt him watching, because she looked up and smiled, parting her legs a little further as if to say, *'come and get it.'* Ray grinned shaking his head. The girl would make a pimp proud.

"Your car will be around momentarily," the blonde announced.

Ray thanked her, then he and the girls went outside and stood in front of the small office building. Moments later, a smile spread across Ray's face as his car rounded the building on the back of a flat-bet wrecker, stopping in front of them.

"Mr. Young?" the driver inquired, stepping down from the cab.

"That's me," Ray answered.

"Usually, we'd let you bring ya' own car around," he explained. "But they got some forensic people round yonder, doing all kinds of stuff." He cast a long glance at Sylvia in her prominently seductive outfit before asking Ray, "Do you have spare keys?"

"What happened to the regular set?" Ray asked, sticking to the script, just in case they didn't take James' word, and intended to use this as a self-incriminating tactic.

"I just checked the log book," he said. "It shows your car received without keys."

"Well, I brought the spare set."

"Okay, let's get you on your way," the man stated as he militated the gears to adjust the bed. He reached inside the window and put the car in neutral. Then he lowered it to the ground by the chain affixed to the front axle.

Ray was opening the driver's door as soon as all four tires were on the pavement, but he noticed something was amiss the moment he sat in the driver's seat to put the car in park. His radio was missing!

"Where's my radio?" Ray asked bolting from the seat and looking down at the man, who was unhooking the chain.

"I wish I could tell ya," he said, getting up off the ground. "We have a policy which excludes us from being responsible for personal property such as—"

"*Somebody's* responsible for my radio!" Ray retorted. "Somebody better tell me *something!*"

"Baby, calm down," Sylvia cooed, wrapping an arm around his waist and kissing him on the jaw. "He may not know what happened to it."

"Somebody knows," he stated in a more composed tone.

"What's the SOP for something like this?" Sylvia asked the man.

"He could file an incident report wit' our sec'tary."

"You wanna do that baby?" she asked Ray.

"Word to the wise," the man spoke before Ray could. "If ya don't have proof of purchase, you'd be makin' an invalid claim."

Ray knew he didn't have proof of purchase. Hell, there was no telling whose car B.J. had stolen the system from, but Ray knew one thing, he didn't steal the damn receipt!

"Let's bounce!" Ray told Sylvia.

\*\*\*

Ray hadn't said two words to Sylvia since they left the impound and parted ways with Connie, who had plans to convene with Black, once he returned from his son's doctor's appointment.

Now, with the windows up and the A.C. blowing, Ray and Sylvia traveled the highway in silence. Ray's anger had accelerated once he'd realized his Gucci sunglasses were also missing.

"It's boring as hell!" Sylvia broke the ice. "Turn on the radio or something!"

Ray glared at her, but she was smiling, hoping to cheer him up. It didn't work.

"They say music soothes the savage beast," she said. "And right now, you're a savage beast."

Knowing his looks didn't work – no matter how menacing they were – Ray just kept his focus on the road. He didn't know what kind of games she was playing, but she was a few seconds away from being jilted. Okay, maybe not, but she was pushing it!

"You want me to sing you a song, baby?"

"Nope," he answered sternly.

Rejecting his answer, she broke into the chorus of *Janet Jackson's 'If.'* "If I was your girl, all things I'd do to you/I'll make you call out my name, I'll ask you who it belongs to/If I was your woman, those things I'll do to you/but I'm not, so I can't, and I won't/but if I was your girl."

He glanced over to see her smiling from ear to ear like she'd just made a debut on American Idol. The way Ray was feeling, right now, he would be the perfect fill-in for Simon Cowell, because this contestant just sounded like a frog choking on another frog. She must've read his thoughts because her smile quickly faded.

"I know I can't sing!" she asserted angrily. "But I thought you would at least appreciate the fact that I'm trying to cheer you up!"

"I do," he uttered, his eyes still on the road.

"No, the fuck you don't!" She crossed her arms over her chest. "Pull over!"

"Do what!" He looked to see if she was smiling.

She wasn't.

"You heard me, pull over!"

"You mean at the next exit, right?"

"Nope! I mean, right now!"

Reluctantly, Ray initiated his right turn signal and conducted the maneuver. He didn't want them to end like this, and he sure as hell didn't want to leave her on the side of the highway, but this was at her request. Plus, he wasn't in the mood to argue.

Finally docking the shoulder of the highway, Ray stopped the car and looked over at her, waiting for her to slide her feet back into her lime-colored patent leather open-toed shoes and walk out of his life. Instead, she pulled her skirt up and peeled off her thong, tossing it into his lap. The gesture confused him, but while he was trying to gather his thoughts, she reinstated her American Idol smile and climbed between the seats to the rear, where she laid with her head rested on the door behind the front passenger seat.

"What are you waiting on?" she asked.

"Girl, I know you don't think we—"

"Yes, we are!" She cut him off, no longer smiling. "You owe me!"

"For what?"

"For getting me upset when I was only trying to cheer you up!" she spoke as if she was twelve, instead of twenty-one. "You hurt my feelings and didn't even apologize. You owe me!"

"Well, can I at least—"

"Nope!" she cut him off again. "Right here— right now!"

Truth be told, he wanted her just as bad as she wanted him, but not on that dangerous highway. He looked through the back window at the oncoming vehicles. The tractor-trailer approaching captured his full attention. The car rocked on its axles as the truck roared by.

"This spot is too dangerous, shawty," Ray protested.

"Mmm!" She moaned, with her eyes closed and two fingers inside her.

She had started without him!

"You heard me?" he asked.

"Shut up!" she responded, eyes still closed. "With your scary ass!"

'No, she didn't,' he thought, putting the car in park.

He'd always heard older cats express how a piece of pussy could get a man killed. Well, that must be his fate, because he was about to pull a death-defying stunt for the pussy awaiting him in his back seat. After shedding his shorts and boxers, Ray climbed into the back seat, positioning himself between Sylvia's legs.

"That's what I'm talking about!" Sylvia voiced, stroking Ray's half-erected penis, causing it to enlarge in her hand. "Ooh, baby! Hurry up and stick it in."

"Damn!"

"What?" she sounded exasperated.

"We may have to postpone this," he told her.

"Why?"

"I don't have a condom."

"Don't worry about that," she said, opening her legs wider. "I trust you."

Playa Ray

## CHAPTER 12

It was well after 6 p.m. when James finally made it up to the fifth floor of the Fulton County Jail. He'd been in intake since five o'clock that morning, and he was bleary. He entered dorm 500-North with two other new arrivals and went directly to the cell he was assigned to, carrying his thin mattress and new hygiene kit. His cellmate wasn't present, so he hefted his mattress and kit on the empty top bunk.

On the desk was an open Bible and a stack of religious pamphlets. On the wall above the desk was a handkerchief with a drawing of a White man with a full beard, who a lot of people like to imagine as Jesus. Looking over the top bunk and out the long and narrow window, James could see the sun setting over the front parking lot as civilians moved to and fro, visiting their loved ones.

This reminded him that he needed to obtain a visitation form and fill it out, immediately. Plus, he had to get on the phone and let Ray know he needed money, being that his money was confiscated, and he had no intentions of trying to survive off jail food, alone. If he'd remembered correctly, fifth floor had store-call on Wednesdays. Therefore, if he could get Ray to come through, tonight, he'd be able to make commissary tomorrow.

"Say, folk?" some guy's voice pulled him from his thoughts.

James turned to face the guy standing in the doorway. "What's up?"

"You ain't bring no cigarettes wit'cha?"

"Nah." One of the guys who came with him had smuggled some in, but James didn't tell him that.

When the guy left, James exited the cell and took in the noisy atmosphere. The loud television, the loud card players; and other dudes who were just being loud for the hell of it. James descended the stairs, ignoring the hard looks thrown in his direction. He was accustomed to Thunder Dorms, and these guys were no more dangerous than he was. Most of them were Followers, who wouldn't burst a grape if they fell on one, without back-up, cowards! James made it to the intercom mounted to the wall by the row of phones that were all occupied and pressed the button.

"What'd you need?" a female's voice boomed over the loudspeakers.

"Some pussy!" somebody blurted out behind him.

"Can I get a visitation request form?" James asked over the laughter the comment had drawn.

"Why didn't you get one at count-time?" she asked.

"I just got here."

"Oh! Come out to the pipe."

The front door mechanically slid open and James exited the dorm, going around to the metal pipe, which was used as a chute to send things up and down in a leather pouch attached to a string. The pouch fell with the form inside. James thanked her, then re-entered the dorm, where he approached one of the guys on one of the four phones.

"Who got that phone after you?" James asked him.

"It's a long line homey," this voice came from behind.

James looked around at the group of men standing in front of the T.V. They were all watching him.

"I didn't hear you," James lied, intending to flush out the leader and separate the shepherd from the sheep. If these clowns thought they were going to delay him from making this important phone call, then they'd better be ready to put on their best circus act.

"I said it's a long line," the guy repeated.

Bingo! James quickly sized him up, he was short about 5'7 or 5'8 and weighed about one-fifty to one-sixty pounds.

"On which phone?" James asked, making direct eye contact with his target, who was about fifteen feet away.

\*\*\*

It had gotten dark by the time Ray pulled into Maple Creek Apartments. After dropping Sylvia off, he called to see if Kim needed a ride to work. She informed him that Patrice had gotten her car fixed. Being that it was still early, and he didn't feel like heading straight home, he made for the self-car wash on Northside Drive. That's when he finally mustered up enough courage to open his trunk and face the music. Well, no music.

His speakers, as well as his amps, were also gone. He had already expected that, so he proceeded to clean and vacuum the large and empty space. Leaving there, he headed to Knight Park to catch a few sales. Fred wasn't home, so Ray conversed with Fred's mother, who was always laughing at everything he said.

"You just tickle me!" she'd always tell him.

Now, entering his apartment, his intentions were to eat, shower and play the Play Station until he was ready for bed. He managed to eat with no interruptions, but as soon as he got in the shower and began to lather up, his cell phone rang. It was on top of the toilet. He drew back the curtain, looking down at the screen. Had it been any other number than the one he was looking at, they would have to answer to his voicemail. He quickly rinsed the soap off his hands and dried them as best he could.

"Hey, baby!" Ray answered it.

"Don't *hey baby*, me!" his grandmother shot back. "You sound like this jailbird I got on the phone."

Ray laughed, knowing she was talking about James.

"Y'all don't call me 'til y'all sittin' in somebody's jail, lookin' like a mule eatin' briar," she continued with one of her favorite phrases, which they always found funny.

"We love you too, Grandma!" James told her.

"Mmm-hmm," she replied. "Y'all better say what y'all gotta say before the time runs out, while y'all runnin' up my phone bill!"

"Yes ma'am," said James. "Ray, I'm on Rice Street."

"Already?"

"Yeah, them folks confiscated my lil' bread and they run store up here tomorrow."

"So, you need me to slide through tonight?"

"If you can. You got your car, right?"

"Yeah, somebody snatched my system tho."

"Nooo!"

"Yeah, they got me. Right now, I'm in the shower. I'll fall through later. How much?"

"They still won't let us go over two-fifty," James told him.

"Gotcha. Anything else?"

"Y'all should be able to visit me Tuesday."

\*\*\*

"I ain't never heard of Bland Town. Where is it at?" James cellmate – who'd introduced himself as Brother Steve asked.

He was sitting on his bunk, sifting through one of his religious books. James was on his own bunk, lying on his back, occasionally glancing out at the lot, hoping to see his brother when he pulled in.

It had been almost two hours since he'd spoken to Ray. The wanna-be gangsters he thought he'd have to fight to make the call, had found out there were cigarettes in the dorm and piled up in the cell where one of the new guys were. One of the men on one of the phones must have gotten a whiff of what was going on because he quickly concluded his call and hurried towards the commotion. James grabbed the vacant phone, not waiting to see who, or if anybody, had next. It didn't matter, because whoever it was, better had been more than trained to go!

"You know where Body Tap is, right?" James now responded to his cellmate.

"Yeah, right over the bridge," he answered.

"If you make a right at the light before you get to Body Tap, that's Huff Road. That's where Bland Town is."

"That's where your brotha's coming from?"

"Nah." James took another gander out at the parking lot. "He's coming from Bolton Road, Ten-Twenty."

Steve became animated. "Man, I got a cousin in Ten-Twenty! He might know her."

"I doubt it."

Why?"

"He don't kick it out there."

"He stays out there, but don't kick it out there?"

88

"Man, my lil bro—" James stopped mid-sentence when he saw Ray's car enter the parking lot. "There he is!" They both watched as Ray parked, got out, and approached the building. "That's my nigga, right there!" James stated proudly.

"Only brotha?"

"Hell yeah! I'll box with God 'bout that nigga! No offense."

"None taken."

"You got a bottle of issued deodorant?"

"Plenty." Steve fetched one. "Here."

James waited until he saw Ray emerge from the building and began rapping on the window with the top of the bottle. Getting to his car, Ray stopped and looked up.

"Blink the lights!" James told Steve.

Steve went over to the switch and flicked the light on and off. James waved. Spotting him, Ray threw up the peace sign, then got into his car and drove off.

***

"Man, these young cats are off the chain!" Steve said, entering the cell and pulling the door back up to alleviate some of the loud noise on the other side.

James found out Steve was thirty years old, from Campbellton Road and was arrested for simple battery on his son's mother for filing child support on him.

"Why'd you say that?" James asked, directing his attention back out the window.

"They robbed the new dude for his cigarettes," Steve answered, flopping down on his bunk. "I'm surprised they didn't jump on him."

"Cause, he didn't put up a fight," James insisted.

"My last cellmate didn't put up a fight when they came in here and took his commissary," said Steve. "They still jumped him."

"You were in here when it went down?" James was now leaning over the bunk, looking down at him.

"I was laying down, reading my Bible," Steve admitted. "They came in with shanks. One of 'em said, *'don't buck if you don't wanna get stuck!'* He was lying on his bunk. They put his store goods in a pillowcase and left. We continued on like nothing happened. 'Bout five minutes later, they came back, snatched him off the bunk, beat him up."

James considered this, but it didn't worry him one bit. He'd been around enough cowards and wanna-be gangsters to know how they operated, and who they'd mess with, but he would still purchase a shank, as soon as the commissary cart arrived. He wasn't adept with his hands like Fred but was a nigga's worst nightmare with anything capable of drawing blood.

"What you got down there to read?" James asked, changing subjects as he reposed on his back, looking at the ceiling. Steve handed him a book, in which he absently grabbed. Once he realized what it was, he laughed.

Steve asked, "What's so funny?"

"Nothing," James responded. "I just should've known you would hand me some shit like this."

"You atheist?"

"A who?"

"Atheist? A person who don't believe in God."

"I didn't say all that," James defended. "I just don't believe in these fables I be hearing about. Niggas walking on water, turning sticks into snakes 'n shit. I can't go for no shit like that!"

"So, you don't wanna read it?"

"This all you got?"

"That's it."

Looking the Bible over in his hand, James focused on the gold lettering that read: *King James Version.*

"*King James,*" he said pensively.

## CHAPTER 13

Ray didn't know what it was, but he'd awakened this morning, feeling a bit uneasy. His head wasn't hurting, but he was quite dizzy. He decided he would go without breakfast after he'd vomited for the second time. He opted for a cup of Thera-flu and headed out. He noticed he was feeling a lot better when he'd turned off Ashby Street onto Martin Luther King Drive. James' house was right beside the library. There was no driveway, so Ray parked behind a brown Chevy Celebrity that looked as if it should be sitting in someone's junkyard, and he already knew who the car belonged to.

"Hey, big brotha!" Kim beamed when she'd opened the door, embracing him.

"What the move is?" he responded, hugging her and kissing her on the cheek.

"Come on in," she told him. "We're just in here gossiping."

Ray entered to see Patrice and another female sitting on the living room sofa.

"Hey, Ray-Ray!" Patrice spoke, waving and smiling.

"What the move is?"

"Nothing," she answered, eyeing him. "Just chillin', still single."

"Girl shut up!" Kim shot, smiling, while the other woman laughed.

"Shit, I am!" Patrice shot back, not taking her eyes off Ray.

Patrice wasn't bad-looking, but Ray just wasn't into Red-bones, since the last one he'd dated. Who thought she was God's gift to men, which flustered him, because he believed women were Satan's gift to men, ruminating the Adam and Eve tale.

"The jacks work?" Ray asked, noticing the opened box on the table that once contained a phone.

"The jacks work," Kim responded. "But the phone company said it may take forty-eight hours for service. You want the number?"

"I'll get it later," he told her. "I just stopped by to check on you."

"Okay."

"You can't chill for a few minutes?" Patrice asked. "A few hours—months?"

"Not this time," he told her, smiling.

Kim asked, "So, we'll be able to see my baby next Tuesday?"

"Should be. You need anything before I leave?"

"No. I'm cool, big brotha."

\*\*\*

"That'll be eighty-three dollars and forty-seven cents," the female cashier announced to Ray.

He knew he shouldn't be spending money like this, being that he hadn't made any profit since his re-up, but he needed a new pair of frames. Truth was, he was doing all he could to avoid Sylvia. He'd never spent this much time with a female, since Trina. He felt like he'd let his guard down.

No. He knew he'd let his guard down, but how? He knew that all women were alike, trifling, cunning, and deceiving heartbreakers. Is that what he wanted—another heartbreak? No matter what he did, he could not shake her. Somehow, she'd broken through the shield he'd successfully, maintained for innumerable months, but he really liked the girl. Maybe he liked her *too* much. That was the problem.

"Have a nice day, sir!"

Ray put on his new Mark Jacob frames and exited the boutique. He wanted to cop a couple of pairs of K-Swiss but decided against it. Being that his spending cash was low. It was bad enough he was going to have to hit his stash spot to pay next month's rent and utilities. While he was pondering this, his cell phone vibrated. He pulled it from his hip, looking at the screen. Sylvia, this marked the sixth time she'd called today, and the sixth time he'd refused to take her call as he replaced the phone and exited South Dekalb Mall.

\*\*\*

"Ain't no way in hell!" James exclaimed.

He was lying on his bunk, reading the Bible – it was all he had. He just wished he had some potato chips to snack on as he did. They denied his store call, claiming his account was not yet open. Now he had to wait all the way to next week.

"God works in mysterious ways," Steve told him.

Well if God was complicit to this involuntary hunger strike, then James didn't have anything pleasant to say about The Man Upstairs. But, he did manage to cop a shank that resembled an ice pick, from some dude who called himself Boss. James offered to pay him for it next week, but, Boss insisted it was free, however, James intended to pay him anyway.

"What you trippin' on now?" Steve who was also lying on his bunk, reading, now asked.

"Man, you can't tell me," James started. "That this nigga, King Nabu – whatever this nigga's name was – put these niggas in a furnace, heated up seven times than it was supposed to be, and these niggas didn't burn! That shit's science-fiction-like a muthafucka!"

"We can't say that."

"The hell if we can't!" James leaned over the bunk, looking down at Steve. "So, if I put you in a furnace—"

"I'll burn," Steve cut him off.

"More like cremate," James stated, laughing as he rolled back onto his back. "But I fuck with them cats Meshach, Shadrach and—"

"Abednego?"

"Yeah, some shit like that," James said. "Them niggas wouldn't bow down for shit! They remind me of me and my niggas. One go to the furnace, the whole clique go to the furnace, straight up!"

\*\*\*

That Friday night, after the crew had stayed down in the trap all evening, they agreed to visit Club 321 on MLK. Ray had managed to dodge Sylvia for three whole days. She hadn't called today, but from Wednesday to Thursday, she'd called seventeen times and left twelve angry messages. He'd only listened to four, but he was sure the other eight were similar.

Ray had given Black the heads up on the situation, considering he was messing with her friend, just in case she feigned damsel in distress to acquire his cell phone. The girl was sharp, so it was undoubted that she would attempt such an exploit. He just hoped like hell she didn't plan to hit Club 321, tonight. At least not this one!

The club was packed. Fred and Ray had copped a table and just watched the crowd – especially Black, who was out on the floor with a Corona in his hand, grinding on every female who was backing it up. Fred had never been the dancing type. If you saw him dance, then you were guaranteed to see pigs fly, and a cold day in hell. Now Ray wasn't the *ragtop – don't stop – get it – get it – type,* but he would periodically get out there, bounce around, grind on the ladies and throw a couple of elbows. Right now, he just wasn't up for it.

Well, that was until *Lil Jon and the Eastside Boyz 'I Don't Give A Fuck'* came pumping through the speakers. Ray bolted from his seat, almost knocking over the small table as he energetically bounced towards the dance floor with his hands up, chiming with – damn near the whole club – as they chanted, "I don't give a fuck!"

Fred couldn't help but smile at his comrades. Yesterday he'd promised Tee he would chill with her tonight, but when Ray and Black mentioned how long it had been since they'd been to the club together, and decided to do so tonight, Fred could not pass it up. He had never put a bitch before his homies and didn't plan on doing it tonight.

It was beyond twelve o'clock. She usually would have called him by now, talking nonsense. Perhaps she was doing something else with her mouth at this moment. He was only putting up with her until the fetus reached fruition for an abortion. She was going to have the abortion, or else!

\*\*\*

Sunday had come around faster than Ray expected. Saturday was like a blur in his memory, although he'd slept most of the day, and there were no calls from Sylvia. When Ray pulled up to his mother's house, he saw the blue Cadillac Seville, indicating that Robert would be joining them for dinner. He'd pretty much expected that. What he didn't expect was to be introduced to another stranger.

"Ray, this is my son, Raymond." Robert did the honors.

Ray quickly conceded that Raymond wasn't the street type. He was brown-skinned with a low haircut. They were both pretty much the same size and height.

Raymond extended his hand. "Nice to meet you."

"Likewise," Ray shook his hand.

\*\*\*

"This seems like a nice neighborhood," Raymond commented. "Real quiet."

Dinner had gone well. Ray found out that Raymond was twenty-three years old and worked with his father at Triple-A Towing. He'd been a member of Hillside Baptist Church since he was born, being that his parents were members, years before he was thought about. He and Robert invited Ray to join them one Sunday. After dinner, his mother insisted he show Raymond around the neighborhood. *'Ain't nothing out there to see,'* was what he'd wanted to say, but he figured she wanted to spend some time alone with Robert.

Now, he and Raymond were walking along The Field, which was a street that curved like a vast horseshoe, lined with industrial warehouses that were all closed on Sundays.

"Yeah, it's quiet on the weekends," Ray now replied.

"It's real noisy on the weekdays?" Raymond inquired.

"These warehouses be in full effect on the weekdays," Ray told him. "I won't say it's real noisy, but you'll know it's a weekday."

"And you grew up out here?"

"Yeah."

"It had to be better than growing up in Lakewood Village."

Ray was surprised. "That's where you grew up?"

"Yeah," answered Raymond. "We moved when I was seventeen. After I was almost killed in a shoot-out."

"Almost?"

"Yeah! The girl I was seeing at the time, got hit. We were standing beside each other when it happened."

Ray looked at him. "Did she make it?"

"She made it to the hospital, but she died before they could get her to the Emergency Room."

"I remember that shooting, ninety-six, right?"

"Yeah."

"Six died— six wounded, ninety-six. They called it the *Triple Six Shooting*."

"Yeah, we moved a week later."

"Hold on," Ray said and answered his cell phone. "Yeah?"

"You still eating?" B.J. asked.

"Nah."

"Come outside."

"I am outside."

"Where?"

"Round the field. Where you at?"

"On my way."

Minutes after Ray hung up, he heard the distant sound of B.J.'s sound system as he rounded the horseshoe. As he stopped in front of them, he muted the system and lowered the front passenger window. T-Roc was sitting in the passenger seat.

"What's up, Ray!" T-Roc spoke.

"What it is, lil homie?" Ray gave him dap. "You aight?"

"Yeah, I'm chillin'."

"That's what's up," said Ray. "Talk to me, B."

"Step into my office," B.J. told him, rolling the window back up.

Ray climbed in behind T-Roc, frowning from the weed smoke that permeated the interior.

"Man, you know I don't smoke," Ray reminded.

"Yeah, I know you got them baby-ass lungs," B.J. joked. "You'll be aight for a few minutes."

Ray said nothing.

"Who is that?" B.J. asked, looking out at Raymond, who was standing with his hands in his pockets.

"Mom's got a new boyfriend."

"That's him?" B.J. asked astonished.

"Hell no, that's his son!"

"Oh!"

"So, what the move is?"

"They had the lil homie's funeral today," B.J. updated.

"Y'all went?"

"T-Roc did."

"What about the girl?"

"I think they had hers yesterday."

"It was yesterday," T-Roc confirmed.

"You went to hers, too?" Ray inquired.

"Yeah, I paid my respects."

"Well, at least *somebody* did!" Ray said, shooting an accusing look at the back of B.J.'s head.

B.J. must've felt it because he turned abruptly in his seat to meet Ray's stare. "Nigga, I don't like funerals either!" he spat. "Thanks to you!"

"Don't blame me for that shit!"

"Nigga, I'll put that smoke pole on your Doberman pinscher – looking ass!" B.J. said sparking laughter.

"So, what y'all boys got planned for tonight?" Ray asked, re-membering he had Raymond waiting outside the car.

"That's what I came through about," B.J. answered. "You got plans for tonight?"

"Nah."

"Well, I found a nice lick," B.J. told him. "We can both get rimmed up, *tonight!*"

\*\*\*

After B.J. left, Ray escorted Raymond back to his mother's house, then excused himself. He had an appointment with Eric to re-up on his product. After leaving Eric's house, Ray headed home to prepare for the mission. It was only a few minutes after eight, and B.J. had planned to pick him up at ten. Ray figured he may as well go ahead and cut and bag up the product. It was well after nine when he'd completed that task. Therefore, he went on and donned the black cargo pants and a turtleneck sweater. He placed his black gloves and ski mask in separate cargo pockets and made for the living room, peering through the curtains.

He didn't see anyone out, milling around, which was a good thing. He just wanted to make a subtle exit and re-entry. B.J. swore that he had a few throw-away Glocks, just in case it got ugly.

*'Things like that come with the territory,'* Ray thought.

He was still livid about his sound system, so he was highly determined to carry out his task, no matter what actions had to be taken. Ray spotted a gray Chevy Lumina pull into the parking lot that was about fifty yards out from his apartment. Seconds later, his cell phone vibrated.

"No doubt," he said through the phone, then cut it off and threw it on the sofa.

He made his exit, locking the door with the only key he was carrying with him. He'd never taken anything on a lick that could be used as a means to identify him. Just in case it got ugly.

"Put'cha gloves on," B.J., who was seated in the front passenger seat told Ray as soon as he'd climbed in the back seat.

Ray donned his gloves. B.J. handed him a black Glock.

"Is it hot?" Ray asked, inspecting the piece.

"I wouldn't doubt it," B.J. answered, then looked over at T-Roc, who was behind the wheel. "Let's ride."

*** 

"Shit, I already know they're gonna find me guilty of that shit," Boss stated to James, impassively. "They got all the evidence they need."

They were in Boss' cell. He was sitting on the bottom bunk and James was perched on the edge of the tiled sink. Boss was twenty-two-years-old, with the face and build of a fifteen-year-old, being that he was about 5'6" and one-hundred thirty-two pounds. He was arrested for murder and had been incarcerated for seven months, awaiting trial.

James found himself liking the little dude because he had heart and was an individualist. Plus, if anybody needed a shank, he was the man to see.

"Ain't no way around it?" James asked. "I mean, if you had a good ass lawyer, you don't—"

"If he could make the evidence disappear," Boss cut in. "Other than that, I'ma ride this shit out like a soldier. I knew the consequences before I pulled the trigger— *fourteen times!*"

As if on cue, the door swung open and Boss' cellmate entered for the umpteenth time to fumble with a stack of papers on one of the shelves under the bunks. Boss glared at him with agitation written all over his face.

"Nigga, why the fuck you keep coming in and out the room like that!" Boss asked his cellmate, who was a little bigger, but younger than him.

"I'm looking for something," he responded, disregarding Boss as he continued fussing with the contents.

"Nigga, you've been in this bitch a million times and ain't left out with shit!" Boss spat.

"I guess I ain't found it yet," his cellmate replied, with malice in his voice as he exited the cell.

"He'll fuck around and be my next victim!" Boss asserted, clearly referring to the guy he'd stabbed on the seventh floor, and another on the sixth, which was why he was now on the fifth floor.

"Isn't he affiliated with that fake-ass mafia out there?" James asked, referring to the group he thought he'd have to bang with over the phone.

"Man, them niggas won't fuck with a picture of me!" Boss spat. "They know my reputation, act stupid if they want to!"

James relished the kid's fortitude. He was a wolf in sheep's clothing. He wished he could get Boss out of his situation and introduce him to the crew. They would immediately take him in. Hell, he needed more cats like Boss on this side to participate in the machination he'd been devising for when he returned to the streets. Whenever that would be.

*** 

T-Roc was pushing the car along a dark two-lane street, where their car was the only one visible. B.J. had gone over the plans with Ray, at least, four times, but Ray was still shaky about the part where T-Roc dropped them off and headed back to Atlanta. Ray couldn't remember a time when B.J. had composed any plans, but since this was his lick, and Ray didn't know anything about anything to contradict any parts of the play, he had no choice but to trust B.J.'s judgment. He still remained skeptical about being abandoned.

"There it is," B.J. finally said.

"I see it," T-Roc replied, decelerating the car that already felt as if it was doing five miles per hour.

"You got enough gas, so you don't have to make no stops?" B.J. told T-Roc once the car came to a halt. "Get to the spot and chill til' we get there."

T-Roc pulled off as soon as they'd dismounted. As they stood there watching the Lumina make its way up the dark road, Ray looked around, trying to see what they had spotted, when all he could see was a gamut of trees on both sides of the road. He was about to ask B.J. when he'd finally spotted a large tree with what appeared to be bright-colored paint at the trunk of it. Inquisitive, Ray walked across the street to get a better look. For some reason, he was not surprised to see that somebody had drawn a stick-man figure with a smiling face, in orange spray paint.

"Now, whose bright idea was this?" he asked B.J.

"T-Roc did that kindergarten-ass shit!" B.J. said, approaching. "You ready?"

"Lead the way."

B.J. produced a small flashlight and started through the dark range of trees, followed by Ray, who immediately drew his gun, not knowing what or who to expect amidst the forest like setting.

Shortly, B.J.'s flashlight went dead.

"Man, I know you didn't come out here with some dead ass batteries!" Ray scolded.

"Nah," B.J. answered. "We're close to the house."

Ray looked ahead of the darkness and could see patches of light shining from the back porches of houses that were still like ghostly shadows from where they were, but the house they were particularly approaching, didn't have on its porch light.

"This must be it?" Ray asked.

"Yeah," answered B.J. "I unscrewed the light last night."

"And what makes you think dudes not at home with his wife and daughter on a Sunday night?"

"Man, just trust me on this!" B.J. told him. "You think I'll have us on a suicide mission?"

Ray thought about what James said about B.J. getting him knocked off on some bullshit and almost said 'yeah,' but instead, he asked, "And you're one-hundred percent sure they don't have dogs?"

"More likely ninety-five percent."

Ray was about to inquire clarification of that answer when B.J. said, "Come on!" and scuttled across the small lawn.

Ray followed suit until they were standing with their backs against the back of the house. B.J. checked his watch.

"We late?" Ray asked.

B.J. didn't answer. Well, he didn't have to because, as soon as the words left Ray's mouth, they heard the sounds of an approaching vehicle, and saw the sudden flash of headlights. From the sound of the vehicle and the flash of its headlights, they could tell the car had pulled into the driveway.

As soon as they heard the whirring sounds of the garage door opening, B.J. drew his gun and looked at Ray, who donned his mask in response. The sound of the garage door closing was their cue to engage, so when they heard the machine pause, then start back up, B.J. donned his mask and dashed around the side of the house, with Ray at his heels.

Getting to the front of the house, they ducked under the half-closed garage door. The guy was still sitting in his blue Chevy Caprice that was parked beside a champagne-colored Cadillac Deville, and as B.J. had assured, they were both sitting on chrome twenty-two-inch rims.

"You can leave it running!" B.J. told the man, shoving the gun in his face. "We can make this quick and easy, or long and hard, you choose."

Ray had taken position by the door as planned, just in case the wife decided to come out and greet her husband. Ray kept an eye on the scene that was playing out in front of him. B.J. had opened the door to let the man out of the car.

"Just don't hurt my wife and daughter!" the man pleaded as he exited the car, hands raised above his head.

"We won't if you cooperate," B.J. told him.

"What y'all want?"

"First, I want you to lay down in front of the car."

The man complied, B.J. tucked his gun, pulled out a roll of duct tape, and bonded the man's hands and feet.

"Now," B.J. said, standing. "Where are the keys to the Cadillac?"

"I got the spare keys on my key ring."

"In the Chevy?"

"Yeah."

"Alarm box?"

"Keyring."

"Killswitch?"

"Ain't none."

B.J. went over to the Chevy, reached into the window, killed the engine, and extracted the keys. Detaching the keys to the Cadillac, he pressed a button on the small box, and the Cadillac's engine came to life. He then tossed the keys to Ray.

"Let's ride!"

## CHAPTER 14

James was lying on his bunk looking out at the parking lot, watching visitors come and go. It was Tuesday, so that meant Ray would be bringing Kim to see him. He didn't know what time they would arrive, but he knew Kim had to be at work at four, and it was after ten, close to the last visit until they started back up at three thirty.

He was about to redirect his attention when he spotted a black Delta Eighty-Eight coming down the narrow road leading to the lot. If it wasn't for the chrome wheels and tinted windows, James would've thought it was his brother, but out of curiosity, he kept his eyes on the car as it found a parking spot. Immediately, the front passenger door swung open, and Kim emerged, walking hastily towards the building. Seconds later, the driver got out, clad in blue shorts, a shirt, and a matching Kangol hat. James didn't think there were too many dudes in Atlanta who drove a black Delta Eighty-Eight and wore Kangols.

"Ha, my nigga done mounted up on them folks!" James said to Steve, who was sitting on his bunk.

"Oh yeah?" Steve was now looking out. "That's him in the blue?"

"Yeah."

"What he got some rims on the whip?"

"Hell yeah, B.J. must've come through."

It took almost thirty minutes for them to announce his visit and almost five more minutes before the visitors arrived on the floor. James and other inmates were standing outside the visitation booth, awaiting their visitors. As they got off the elevator, some visitors branched off to the southside. James spotted Kim, but no Ray.

"Where's Ray?" James asked as soon as he entered one of the doorless booths. He had to lean closer to see her through the steel grate that had a multitude of pencil-sized holes wedged between the two and thick Plexiglass windows on each side.

"Oh, I'm fine!" she said, taking a seat. "Thanks for asking!"

"My bad, baby," he apologized, felling a bit asinine. "I saw y'all pull-up."

"He's downstairs," she said with much attitude, crossing her arms over her chest. "He's coming back with Fred and Black later."

"Oh!" He took a seat on the steel stool, resting his forearms on the protruded slab of concrete. "I miss you."

"I miss you, too," she said, with attitude still lingering.

James was happy to see his sweetheart, but he wasn't in the mood for her attitude whether he'd piqued it or not. He leaned closer to get a better look at her. She was pouting, with her eyes to the ceiling.

"You should've stayed your ass at home with that lil' girl shit!" he fussed.

"I might as well have!" she snapped. "It seems like you were expecting, Ray, anyway!"

"That's not true," he assured meekly, hoping to diminish the verbal dispute that seemed imminent. "I miss you— I miss him also. I just thought he was coming up with you, that's all. I'm sorry, forgive me?"

"I'll think about it."

"That'll work," he said. "So, how's my baby?"

"I'm fine."

"Everything okay at the crib?"

"Yep, we got a house phone. You got a pen and paper?"

"Nah, hold on."

He exited the booth to see if any of the other guys had the implements. The guys in the first two booths didn't have the items. He was about to ask the guy in the third booth, but quickly detoured when he saw the guy with his pants down to his ankles, masturbating off to the girl on the other side, who was bent over with her pants down. The guy was so caught up in the moment, he didn't bother looking back to make sure it wasn't an officer who'd stumbled upon him. James obtained the necessities from the guy in the next booth, jotted the house number down, then returned the pen.

"Is Ray taking you to work?" James asked Kim, upon returning to the booth.

"He's gonna drop me off at home and go get his hair braided," she answered. "Patrice got her car fixed."

"Okay," he said. "Well, he's gonna help you out on the bills 'n stuff."

"And how long do you think you're gonna be in here?"

"I can't say," he answered. "You know how slow Fulton County is."

"Uh-huh."

Something wasn't right. James had been with Kim long enough to know when something was bothering her. He felt like she was about to drop a bomb on him. A bomb he was not yet prepared for, but whatever it was, he knew it was impending, and it was best to go ahead and get it over with.

"Look, Kim," James started, preparing himself for the worse. "Whatever it is, you need to tell me. Stop beating around the bush and come on with it."

***

In the parking lot, Ray was sitting on the trunk of his car with the engine running and music low, playing *Eminem's 'Superman.'* He was holding the remote that controlled the new sound system and 10-disc CD changer. Yesterday, he'd gotten up early to have it installed. The place also sold rims and tires, so Ray got his car aligned and let them put the rims on and the tinted they windows for free.

Ray had spent a nice piece of change, but it was worth it. Besides, B.J. had found seven ounces of weed and fifty-eight hundred dollars in the Chevy. That made them wish they'd ventured inside the house, looking for more, but since the job went well and everything was split three ways, everyone was content.

Now, Ray looked at the gold Embassy watch on his arm he'd found in the Cadillac, and calculated that visitation should be over in about ten minutes. But when he looked towards the building, he saw Kim storming out the front door, with her pocketbook violently swinging in one hand, both hands balled into fists, and her face furiously contorted.

"Fuck!" she cried out, loud enough to be heard throughout the parking lot as she stumbled, breaking one of her heels.

She stopped long enough to snatch both shoes off and hurl them to the ground, then resumed her menacing stride towards the car. Ray saw the tears welling up in her eyes as she passed him and climbed into the car, slamming the door.

"That damn Ike and Tina can't have a good day for shit!" Ray reflected as he slid off the trunk to collect the shoes and damaged heel.

When he got into the car and placed the shoes and heel at her feet, he saw that Kim was crying, with her face buried in her hands. He wanted to ask her what was wrong, but he had a feeling he'd find out later.

***

"Boy, you owe me extra for this!" Tasha told Ray as she rinsed shampoo out of his hair at the kitchen sink. "You had all weekend to take this wool down and wash it!"

"I told you, I been busy," Ray's voice resounded from the bottom of the sink.

"Yeah, chasing them nothing-ass hoes!"

Ray knew better than to go there with her. She had already made it clear that she wanted him. In fact, she made sure he was aware of it, every time he came to get his hair braided. He'd even had sex with her, once. That day, he'd fallen asleep, sitting between her legs while she was braiding his hair. When she finished, she woke him up and told him he could take a nap in her bed. Being that he was feeling quite spent and didn't have anywhere to go, he took her up on her offer.

When he awoke, it was almost dark outside. Lying beside him, on her side, propped up on one elbow and smiling was Tasha. The scene was a bit uncanny, but what really surprised him was the fact that she was clad in her birthday suit – or, as Bernie Mac would say: buck-ed naked!

The sex was good, but Ray couldn't see it being consistent. He thought, Tasha was a cool individual, but she was looking for someone to walk down the aisle with, and the only aisle Ray walked down, was in a grocery store.

"Here!" Tasha draped a towel around his neck. "You can dry your own rug."

Ray lifted his head from the sink in time to see Tasha's wide ass and hips bulging through her jeans as she sauntered out the kitchen. Ray dried his hair as he entered the living room, where Tasha was already seated on the sofa with a pillow on the floor in front of her.

"You want your braids like A.I.?" she asked, referring to the basketball player, *Allen Iverson.*

"Hell no!" he replied, taking the towel through his legs like it was a basketball, crossing it over, then tossing it at the recliner in the form of a lay-up. "I want my shit like Ray-I!"

*** 

It was shortly after five o'clock when Ray pulled into the jail's parking lot with the windows down and music up as Dirty's 'Hit Da Flo' sounded off through the speakers. Fred and Black were already there, sitting on the hood of Fred's car. Ray pulled up on them, turning the music down.

"Awww shit!" Black exclaimed, jumping off the car with his fist to his mouth, checking out Ray's car. "This nigga done snapped!"

Fred was smiling. "That's right, stunt on they ass!"

"Shit, I ain't making no noise," Ray replied. "Let me park this bullshit, so we can head on in."

"Man go 'head with that aggravated-flexing!" Black joked.

Ray laughed as he drove off to find a parking spot. Fred and Black were standing by his car by the time he'd applied the new steel security collar over the steering column.

"Nobody's gonna steal your car from in front of the jail!" Black said when he saw the collar.

Ray didn't respond.

"So, B.J. finally came through, huh?" Fred asked as they trooped towards the building.

"Yeah, he put me on," Ray answered. "He snatched him a pair too."

"Tell him to fuck with me," Fred told him.

"I'll do that."

After they signed in, it took about thirty minutes for them to be called to go up.

"What up, Pimps, Playas and Gangstas!" James greeted as they entered the booth.

Fred sat the plastic chair outside the booth, so they would have more room in the small space that was a few centimeters bigger than a telephone booth.

"Boy, you fallin' off in this bitch!" Ray laughed. "You look like that nigga Pookie on New Jack City!"

They all erupted with laughter.

"Oh, you're on the bullshit!" James said.

"Nah, straight up, right," Ray persisted. "J.J. from Good Times said he wants his pants back."

"Damn, Jay!" Black exclaimed through his laughter. "Get that nigga up off you!"

"I can't do nothing with him," James admitted.

"If you stay in here too long," Ray continued. "You'll be looking like that shampoo, *Head 'N Shoulders!*"

They enjoyed that laugh for a long time.

"So, how you wanna handle this?" Fred asked once everybody was sober from the laugh attack.

"If I get a bond, it'll be high," James said. "Even if it's paid, I'll still need a lawyer. I'd rather have a lawyer and ride it out for a few months.

"So, you're gonna take it to trial?" Ray asked.

"Hell yeah!" James answered. "They didn't find that shit on me!"

Ray asked, "What the stash look like?"

"A lil' over three stacks."

"Did they say anything about the gun?"

"Nothing."

"Fuck that!" Black spoke up. "We need to go ahead and pop that shit off! That way, we can get you a lawyer, and bail you out. Then we can go ahead and—" Black broke off when he saw the look Fred was giving him. Ray saw it but maintained his innocence.

"You got the number to the house?" Ray asked, feigning slow to what he'd just witnessed.

"Yeah, Kim gave it to me," James answered, then asked Ray for a few minutes with Fred and Black.

Exiting the booth, Ray walked towards the elevators, stopped short of them, and leaned his back against the wall. Ray wasn't stupid by a long shot. He knew from the day Fred had shown them the new guns that something was about to go down. They didn't let him in on it, so he figured they didn't think he was capable of pulling off whatever they'd planned, considering he'd never told them about the first lick with B.J. and didn't plan on telling them about the recent one.

While he waited, he could hear the indistinctive chatter of the visitors, except for one who he could make out, who was loud and pretty much angry.

"You should've thought about that while you were out there fucking them nasty-ass hoes behind my back!" the female vented.

"And I bet neither one of those hoes been up here to check on your stupid ass. Or even thought about putting two cents on your books! Cause if they did, your broke ass wouldn't be begging *me* for money!"

'*The way women talk to men when they're locked up,*' Ray thought.

He seriously doubted that she would've said any of those things to him if he was out, but then again, there are some bold-ass women and some weak-ass men in the world.

"Fuck you, ol' small-dick bastard!" the female shouted, then marched out of the booth, headed for the elevators.

Apparently, everyone had heard the outburst, because they were all including Black and Fred looking back to see who was putting their foot down. The girl was cute, but she was too small to talk to *anyone* like that.

She didn't even look in Ray's direction as she approached the elevators. Seconds after she'd gotten on, Fred and Black emerged from the booth.

"Y'all gone?" Ray asked.

"I gotta get back to the trap," Black answered.

Fred said, "I'ma drop him off and stop by Eric's crib."

"I guess I'll get up with y'all later," Ray told them.

"Make sure you get at B.J. for me," Fred reminded.

They dapped as the elevator arrived. Once they got on, Ray headed back to the booth, where he pulled the chair back inside and sat in it.

"Everything aight?" he asked.

"Yeah, everything's straight," James answered. "I see you done stepped it up on the whip."

"B.J. hooked it up."

"I had already figured that. How's mama doin'?"

"She's happy," Ray answered. "She'll be down here Saturday."

"Man, you make sure you keep an eye on that nigga!"

"She's good," Ray answered. "What's the deal with you and Kim?"

"What'd she tell, you?"

"Nothing."

"She told me some off-the-wall-ass shit."

"And what was that?"

"She's pregnant."

Ray made a face. "How is that *off-the-wall?*"

"Cause, it's not mine."

"So, whose is it—hers?" Ray quipped.

"The baby's not mine, Ray!"

"So, you think Kim's been—"

"You don't think she would?" James cut his brother off.

Ray had to really consider that because he'd never pictured Kim in that light before. Maybe because he looked at her like a sister.

That may be the reason why he'd failed to view her the same as he did other women. So, perhaps James was right.

Playa Ray

## CHAPTER 15

"What made you blurt that shit out in front of Ray like that?" Fred asked Black. They were entering downtown via Marietta Street, and slowly moving amid the evening traffic.

"To be honest," Black answered, "I had forgot all about that shit, but, Ray ain't stupid."

"We both know that," Fred told him. "But we agreed not to mention it to him, or in his presence."

"Shit, I forgot," Black repeated. "James wants us to wait until he gets out, but nobody knows when that'll be. I'm ready to step this nickel-and-dime bullshit up. I can't even take Nikki and the kids on a decent shopping spree, without worrying about spending the rent money. Plus, I'm trying to move out of Capital Homes, like yesterday!"

"Yeah, I feel that," Fred said, and he really did.

He'd asked Eric to put him on the lick for a reason, to get paid! He never thought his plans would be hampered, due to the incarceration of one of his partners. He too was tired of peddling crumbs. Just last night, he'd spent over two hours casing out the spot. All the while, considering bringing it to Ray's attention, and even including D.J. as a fourth man. James had good intentions, but Fred didn't feel like James' intentions were enough to remit the task – not to mention his future.

"What's up?" Black answered his cell phone.

"Hey, sexy chocolate!" Connie purred through the phone.

"Shit, that's an understatement!" Black responded.

She laughed. "Oh, you're just too conceited!"

"Damn right!" Black boasted. "What's up wit'cha?"

"Nothing, hoping to get lucky."

"It won't be today, shawty," he told her. "I gotta handle some things."

"I understand," she said. "How about tomorrow?"

"We can work that."

"Okay, I'll see you then."

"Aight." Black ended the call.

"That was shawty from Chapel Forest?" Fred inquired.

"Yeah."

"She won't let you make money out her spot?"

"I never asked."

"She knows what you do, right?"

"She should."

"Shit, that might be a nice lil trap spot," Fred told him. "That's the only reason I fuck with those project chicks, to trap out they shit."

Fred pulled up to Black's apartment, where Nikki was sitting on the porch, holding Lil Keith, and talking to the next-door neighbor, while Nicole played patty-cake with the neighbor's daughter at the bottom of the steps.

Black sat there watching his lovely family. He had four children and was barely taking care of them. It's a wonder that Felicia and Danielle had not filed for child support on him – although Danielle had moved to Virginia with some White man, taking his two-year-old daughter with her. Black kept in touch and sent what he could, although Danielle insisted that she and Denise were well taken care of.

"Black!" Fred called, pulling him from his reverie.

"What's up?" he asked, facing Fred.

"You a'ight?"

"Hell no!" Black answered, pushing the door open and getting out. "I won't be a'ight til' we make that shit happen!" Black slammed the door and walked away before Fred could respond.

Fred knew exactly what he meant, and their sentiments were mutual.

***

"Man, you're still in here tripping on that shit?" Boss asked, entering James' cell carrying a large manila envelope.

"That shit got a nigga faded," James answered. He was lying on his bunk, staring at the ceiling. Steve wasn't in the cell.

"Only if you *let* it fade you," Boss told him. "But I brought you something that might cheer you up."

Boss handed him the envelope, and James extracted a Black Tails magazine from it. He shot a blank look at Boss, who was smiling at him.

"It works for me," Boss told him. "And don't start that fresh-off-the-street shit. I jacked my dick on my first night in this bitch."

"This you?" James asked, slowly turning the pages.

"Of course," he answered. "I be charging these niggas to use my shit. Your roommate, too."

James shot another look at Boss.

"Oh, don't let him fool you with that holier-than-thou shit!" Boss said. "He's human."

James could do nothing but laugh at his new-found friend, who never failed to amuse him.

"Oh, yeah," Boss pulled a small bottle of lotion from his sock, placing it on the desk. "Can't go in without the kit."

James looked down at the bottle, but before he could protest if that was what he really intended to do, Boss was on his way out the door.

"Take ya time," Boss said, then pulled the door up, locking it.

James reverted back to the magazine. As he continued to turn the pages, he felt himself becoming aroused with every picture. By the time he'd neared the end of the book, he was fully erected.

There was no turning back now!

\*\*\*

After leaving the jail, Ray decided to head straight home and take a long, hot bath, being that he didn't have time to wash after sexually paying Tasha for braiding his hair. While driving along Bankhead Highway even when passing Overlook Atlanta all he could think about was Kim. Would she pull such a stunt— *had* she pulled such a stunt?

The situation had him baffled. After receiving his order from the drive-thru at Checkers, he resumed his drive down Bankhead, until he came to the stoplight in front of Bowen Homes. He always hated when this particular light caught him. A slight glimpse of the apartments always brought back bad memories and stirred up the hostility he felt for his supposed half-brother, who lived with his supposed father.

His anger didn't fade until the light turned green, and he'd made it past the truck stop, but he felt more relaxed when he pulled into his apartments. He collected his food and CD case and dismounted. When he approached his door, he noticed a folded piece of paper stuck in the side of his burglar bar door.

"I know these folks ain't trying to kick a nigga out," he said, grabbing the paper, unfolding it.

It was a hand-written letter that read:

*I came by to see how you were doing, but I guess you're with some other skank. Well, it doesn't matter since you don't belong to me. Anyway, call me because we really need to talk. It's Imperative!*

Ray felt as though he should've stayed in school a little longer because he didn't know what the hell imperative meant, but he knew who the note came from. He looked around half expecting to see her standing by, watching him. He entered his apartment, placed his food on the kitchen table and carried the CD case to the living room where he inserted five CDs into the stereo's changer. He selected a track on one of the CDs before heading back to the kitchen to tend to his food. While he was pulling his burger and fries from the bag, *Organization's 'Get That Bitch,'* sounded through the stereo's speakers, and as always, Ray with a mouthful of French fries aided *G-Roc* with the first verse!

"I met this hoe at the Five-Five-Nine, and shawty say that her name's Elaine/her complexion chocolate-rain, say the black bitch dance at the Blue Flame."

\*\*\*

"Did you hear what I said?"

Nikki's voice pulled Black from his abstract musing, for the third time, since they'd been sitting at the dinner table. She had been talking and feeding Lil Keith, who was seated in his high chair. All Black heard was something about a job interview and a babysitter. He was too caught up in his thoughts of getting his paper right and moving his family to a better location, to hear anything else.

"What?" he asked, with agitation in his voice.

Nikki caught an attitude. "I said we need to hurry up and go grocery shopping, cause we're running out of baby food, milk, and pampers. Plus, we need—"

"Every time I turn around, you need something!"

"I didn't say '*I*—*'* she took offense. "I said—"

"It don't matter what the fuck you said!" he spat. "You must think—"

"You better watch your mouth around these kids!" she scoffed, with a look that conveyed murder!

Black looked over at his kids, who were staring back at him, wide-eyed. He didn't mean for them to witness that side of him, but he also didn't apologize for the outrage. Instead, he abruptly got up from the table and headed for the bedroom.

After pocketing his money and drugs, and tucking his gun inside his waistband, he turned and was about to exit, but stopped short of the door where Nikki was standing akimbo in the threshold.

"So, you're just gonna leave like you always do, huh?" she said. "Why can't we talk our problems out like responsible adults? You come home with this attitude and expect for me—"

"Move, Nikki!" he growled in a low tone.

"No!" she protested. "You can't just—"

Black didn't know whether he'd struck or shoved her, but whatever he did, sent her flying backward into the hallway's wall, with her head and back making the negotiation. Her hand quickly shot up to her chest as if to keep her heart from leaping out, while tears from her extensive, frightened eyes, cascaded down her terror-filled face. That's when Black realized he'd done something he never thought he'd do— hurt his baby! But, once again, he did not apologize. He just pushed past her and out the front door.

\*\*\*

After eating and taking a bath, Ray still couldn't get his mind off Kim, so he called her job to check on her. Only to be told that Kim didn't show, nor call with an excuse why she would be absent. It struck him as odd, but she was still a bit distraught when he dropped her off at home from her visit with James. Feeling as though something was wrong, he called both the house and her cell phone to no avail.

Now, he knew enough about women to know how they acted when they were upset, but there were numerous of times when Kim was pissed off at James and wouldn't answer her cell phone when he would call, trying to make amends, but during those times, she *always* answered her phone when Ray called. Knowing that her big brother would always cheer her up. She wasn't answering now!

One time, Ray remembered, during one of Kim's tantrums, she'd threatened to slit her wrist. He hoped that wasn't the case. So, after coercing himself to think optimistically, he redialed her cell and left a message for her to call him back. Then, he continued with his plans, which was to play his Play Station and listen to his old CD's. *Scarface's 'The Diary'* was already in mid-play when he copped a seat on the couch and commenced to playing Resident Evil.

He was almost an hour into his game when his cell phone vibrated on the table. He paused the game and grabbed the phone, expecting to see Kim's name and number on the screen. It wasn't.

"What's up twin!" he greeted his sister, April who was calling from Massachusetts. She was four years younger than him, but they referred to each other as *Twin*, because people always remarked about how much they favored.

"Hey!" she exclaimed. "What's new besides James being arrested?"

"How'd you hear about that?"

"I just got off the phone with mama. Who couldn't hold water if you gave her a cup to hold it in!" April teased.

118

Ray couldn't help but laugh at his baby-sister. Besides features, they also shared a keen sense of humor. She'd also won a few acclaims for being the Class Clown, but unlike her brothers, she'd finished school and allowed them to pay her tuition with the money they saved from hustling. They'd even had enough money to move her into a room at one of the off-campus houses. Now, she was working part-time and maintaining like the truly independent woman they'd hoped she would become.

"She also told me about her new, Giovanni Casanova," April continued. "Any comments?"

"No."

"So, you like him?"

"Pretty much. Why?"

"I was just inquiring."

Ray could never possess where she'd gotten her elocution from. To a person who didn't know her, she would come off to them as a well-educated white girl.

"Speaking of Casanovas," Ray started. "Have you found one?"

"Excuse me!"

"I know you've found somebody by now," he was grinning to himself.

"Are you *that* anxious to become an uncle?"

He almost told her that he was closer than she thought but caught himself. If anyone hears of Kim's baby and James' maybe, it won't be from him.

Instead, he said, "You're at Harvard. I'm quite sure you've met some smart, intelligent dudes up there."

"Smart, intelligent, and corny."

"Corny?"

"Like Carlton on The Fresh Prince of Bel-Air," she snickered.

"These guys are too uppity for me."

"So, you'd rather have a street nigga that ain't 'bout shit?" he asked. "One of them ol' fake-ass thug-niggas who'll get his stupid ass killed or locked up for the rest of his life, leaving you to raise ten kids?"

She was silent on the other end.

"You there?" he asked.

"Every day, I think of how my brothers risked their lives to make sure I was on the right path and not become a statistic," she said. "It would be imprudent not to mention disloyal for me to make it this far and let some poor-excuse-of-a-man ruin my life. It won't happen."

Once again, Ray was proud of his baby sister.

"I'll get my degree," she resumed. "I at least owe y'all that much."

"Well, I'm glad you feel that way."

"It's imperative."

There's that damned word again. It caused him to think about Sylvia. While he was mulling over the contents of her note, his second line beeped. He looked at the screen.

"Say, twin?"

"One of your sweethearts?" April guessed.

"I've never put a chicken head before my family," he professed. "And you know that."

"True," was all she said.

"But I do have to take this call," he told her. "It's important, or should I say, *imperative*?"

She chuckled. "That'll work. I should be able to visit in another month or so. Tell James I love him, and I love you also."

"You know we love and miss you too," he said. "Until next time."

"Until next time."

Ray quickly switched lines. "Kim?"

"Hey big brotha!" she exclaimed, sounding normal.

Perhaps, *too* normal!

"You okay?" he asked.

She sighed. "I'm still upset, but for the most part, I'm cool."

For some odd reason, Ray thought back to the day he'd found out about his ex-girlfriend, Trina, and his half-brother, Mark. He'd called her cell phone to tell her that the car dealership called inquiring about a late payment on her car. She'd given them the number to his cell phone because she was in the process of buying one at the time.

When he didn't get an answer, like he usually would, he called her job, only to be told Trina had called in, complaining to be sick. He knew that the allegations were false but didn't try to dispute the manager. Instead, he thanked the manager, redialed Trina's cellular, and left a brief message: *"Call me when you go on break."*

He hung up as he started his car and exited Wendy's parking lot, where he was working at the time. He'd complained of a migraine, and the manager excused him for the day. It wasn't even five minutes after he'd left the message when Trina called back. Knowing how he was going to play his cards, he simply asked her if she were on break. When she informed that she was, he briskly told her about the call from the dealership and avowed he would see her when he got home. When he hung up, he quickly devised a plot to get back at his lying girlfriend.

But his plot was immediately crushed when he pulled into Allen Temple Apartments and spotted her car. He had an idea what she was doing, but the question was *who* was she doing? Her sneaky ways had already led him to believe she was having sex with God-knows-who.

Ray parked his car and walked dutifully to their apartment then let himself in, ready to accept the inevitable. When he entered, he noticed that his migraine had subsided from the Motrin his manager gave him. He'd noticed Trina emerging from the bedroom, followed by Mark, clearly on their way out. They stopped in their tracks like three deer caught in an array of headlights, though Ray felt more like a raging bull. He was livid but defied to let it show as he deiced the frozen scene by pushing past them to the bedroom, where sex still lingered.

Mark, not being the street type, sagely made his exit, not willing to stick around for any consequences, but Trina re-entered the room, where Ray was gathering his belongings. As if the scene and the phone call wasn't enough evidence, she had the gall to tell him it wasn't what he thought. That they were just talking. Ray just remained silent as he finished packing. He gave her his key and left.

"Well, I was just checking on you," Ray now said to Kim, ready to spring his trap to see if there was a little truth to what James had accused. "I know you're on your break, and I'm not trying to cut into the lil' time they give you."

"Yeah, them lil' thirty minutes be shooting by too quick!" she laughed. "Plus, Donna got me washing dishes, so her fat ass will be hollering my name, right at thirty minutes."

Bingo!

# CHAPTER 16

Still woozy from the night before, Black stirred from his sleep with the headache of the century. He had half-closed eyelids and blurry retinas, as he slowly surveyed the vaguely familiar room, until his eyes fell on what appeared to be the back of a woman, asleep beside him. He noticed that they both appeared to be naked. Suddenly, his thoughts regressed to how Nikki looked after he shoved her into the wall. The thought churned his heart. His arm felt like it was the only thing on his body that functioned properly. He placed his hand on her bare back.

"Nikki?" his voice was low and raspy, which gained him no response. After clearing his throat which was a bit painful, he tried again. "Nikki?"

"I'ma let you have that," the sleepy voice replied.

"Huh!" Black, coming alert, drew his hand back.

It wasn't that he didn't hear what she'd said, he'd heard perfectly clear. It was just that he wasn't sure if *she* was the one who'd said it, but they were the only two in the room.

"You heard me!" she stated, turning to face him. This was not Nikki! "I'ma let you have that," Connie continued. "Just this one time, considering what happened, last night. Plus, you might still be drunk for all I know.

She didn't seem upset at all but did turn her back to him to resume her slumber. Black didn't bother her, instead, he just laid there, staring at the ceiling, trying to place last night's events into a respectable order.

He vividly remembered shoving Nikki into the wall then storming out of the apartment. Everything else was almost strenuous, but he'd managed to slowly retain. Upon leaving the apartment, he went to the trap with the intent to stay out all night until he'd sold the remainder of his product. After an hour of trapping and smoking with the other dealers, he ended up calling Connie to see if she still wanted to get lucky. She did, but it was another hour before he spotted Boston to drop him off.

Meeka and two men were present when he arrived. They were drinking and smoking, but their lack of drugs and alcohol wasn't enough for how he was feeling. Therefore, he chipped in with the two guys and bought an ounce of weed and a fifth of Seagram's Gin. Whatever happened after the alcohol took over, was a blur. He could only conclude that he and Connie had sex, though he couldn't remember participating.

"You got plans for today?" he asked, now regarding her back.

"I had plans last night," she replied, not stirring. "But they were hindered because *somebody* was too drunk to perform."

"Damn, my bad shawty," Black apologized, sliding over and pressing his body into hers. His penis landed between her buttocks, and instantly erected, while he toyed with one of her nipples. "I know you can find it in your heart to give me another chance."

She didn't respond, Black already knew what he had to do, so he rolled her onto her back, and went down on her. Connie moaned as Black lapped at the folds of her pussy like a ravenous dog. It didn't take long before she started gyrating her hips, pretty much indicating that she was now wide awake. Her whole body tensed up when he began sucking on her clit. She didn't have to say it, but Black knew she was about to come when she arched her back.

However, he wasn't letting her off that easy. Intentionally cheating her out of an early orgasm, Black mounted Connie and hoisted her legs up, then put her into the missionary position. The look on her face was half surprised and half amused. Whatever, it was, it had him turned on. Black was thinking of protection, but he was also thinking against it. He was just hoping Connie didn't protest as he guided his dick inside of her and she didn't. Considering this, he took advantage and rammed every inch of his pipe deep into her warm, wet tunnel and put the pound game down on her like a human jackhammer.

After, almost two hours of lovemaking, Connie set out to make breakfast, while Black showered. After they'd eaten, Connie showered, then they rode out to K-Mart.

"Right here," Connie said, stopping in the aisle in front of a basket full of cosmetic items. Black, who was trailing behind, stopped beside her. "It has organic soap, body wash, bubble bath, shampoo, lotion, and massaging cream."

"So, I should get that one?" Black asked.

"Definitely!" She grabbed the basket and started up the aisle. "Now, you need some scented candles and a card that says, *I'm sorry*, or something like that."

Black followed her as she picked out all the things, she felt would avail him when he went home to reconcile with Nikki. He paid for the items, and they were back in the car on their way to Capital Homes. He had her drop him off on Capital Avenue, just in case Nikki was out-and-about.

"Good luck!" Connie said when she brought the car to a halt.

Black looked over at her. All day, she'd been giving him all kinds of advice on how to get back on Nikki's good side. That made him view her in a new light, considering most women would have done the total opposite.

"What you about to do?" he asked.

"Don't worry about me!" she answered, smiling. "You have a heart to unbreak."

He nodded. "You're right, I owe you, big time."

"Dinner and a movie."

"That's what you want?"

"Uh-huh."

"That's a bet."

He leaned over, kissing her passionately, for the first time. Then, grabbing the basket and shopping bag from the back seat, Black got out and headed for his apartment. The first thing he wanted to do was spend some time with the kids before ushering them over to the next-door neighbors to babysit for the night. Then, he would work on Nikki.

When he got to his apartment, he sat the basket on the porch, while he negotiated the lock with his key. He was surprised to see that Nikki wasn't sprawled out on the living room sofa, watching her soap operas. He was more surprised to see the T.V. wasn't even turned on. Perhaps she was too upset to watch T.V.

He locked the door and placed the basket and shopping bag on the coffee table, then made for the bedroom. He immediately noticed that Nikki's array of cosmetics was missing from the dresser. The closet door was left wide open, revealing only his clothes and shoes.

"Man, I know damn well—" he fumed, rushing from the room to the kids' room. Where the only things visible were Nicole's bed and Lil Keith's crib. Infuriated, Black re-entered his bedroom, snatched the cordless from its crib and dialed Nikki's cell phone.

"What?" she answered, nonchalantly.

"Nikki don't do this!" he said, struggling to keep his voice equal to hers. "Come on home so we can work this out."

"It's over, Keith."

*Keith*— they'd been together for over three years and, not once had she ever called him by his first name.

"Nikki, that's the first time I've ever put my hands on you," Black admitted. "I'm sorry."

"It was the first," she replied. "But it may not be the last. I won't allow myself to be in an abusive relationship, and I refuse to put my kids through it."

"Those are my kids too, Nikki," he reminded. "You're just gonna take my kids away from me?"

"I'll arrange for you to see them, once I get situated."

"Where y'all at?"

"I'll arrange for you to see them, once I get situated," she repeated. "This number should be changed by tomorrow."

"So, I can't call and check on them?" he asked, disbelieving to what he was hearing.

"I gotta go Keith."

"Nikki!"

She hung up.

"Fuck!" Black yelled, flinging the phone against the wall, shattering it.

***

"Shit, them niggas will front you whatever you want," Poncho told Fred.

Fred had come to Edgewood with the intent of making money. He'd been in the trap since 12:00 pm, and it was now after 3:00 pm. Michelle didn't get home from work until after four, but she was the last thing on his mind.

"Nah, I ain't trying to do business with them," Fred now responded.

"Man, despite what you heard about those cats, they handle business like it's supposed to be handled," Poncho assured. "If they front you, and you fuck over them. It'll be slow walking and sad singing, but I can put a few words in for you if you're really trying to step it up."

Fred had to really consider that. He'd asked Poncho to put him on to a plug, but he didn't expect to be recommended to the Drop Squad. He also didn't plan on turning to his brother for help. He felt that would be a sign of weakness, considering Eric was so proud of him for doing his own thing.

While he was pondering his response, a car's sound system caught his attention. He looked to see a cherry red Chevy Monte Carlos on chrome wheels pull into the apartments and stop in front of them. The driver muted the stereo and dismounted, but Fred was too focused on the female passenger to regard the driver.

This bitch really gets around, he thought. He couldn't put an exact number on how many men he'd seen or heard of her being with, before, or after Ray had called it quits. He still hadn't told Ray that she'd tried to get at him once, but he didn't feel like he had to since he'd turned her down. Besides, Ray already knew she was a slut. It was just too bad it took him catching her with his half-brother to come to his senses.

Just as Fred was watching her, she was watching him.

"What's up, fellas!" the driver said, approaching.

That's when Fred realized it was Dre, one of Poncho's closest friends that grew up with him in Edgewood. He was the first-person Poncho introduced him to when they first met. Dre sold drugs but was mostly known as a stick-up kid.

"Trying to keep the lights on," Poncho replied, giving his friend dap. "I see you done caught a nigga slipping."

"You know how I do," said Dre. "What's up wit'cha, Fred?"

"Same shit," Fred dapped him. "You know how it is."

"Boy, who you got wit'cha?" Poncho asked.

Dre answered, "some straight rip."

"That's exactly what she is," Fred reflected.

"That bitch looks familiar," said Poncho.

"You might've run across that hoe before," Dre told him. "Me and Lil' Al just G'd her ass!"

"Lil Al from Kirkwood?" Poncho inquired.

"Yeah."

"I ain't seen that fool in a minute. What's he been up to?"

"Man, that crazy ass nigga talking about running off in a bank!"

"He's bullshitting, right?"

"Hell no!"

Listening to this, gave Fred an idea. He'd met Lil Al a while back and knew from the jump that the nigga was down for whatever. Hearing stories of how he and Dre were kicking in drug dealer's doors and leaving the scenes bloodied, if required, gave him confirmation. Now, he was thinking of recruiting these two for the lick to accompany him and Black. That way, he and Black could go ahead and get the ball rolling. This would also exclude Ray like James wanted. Although he'd rather have Ray, than anyone outside the circle. Now, he had to find a way to get Dre and Lil Al together, so he could explain everything to them. That may entail a trip to Kirkwood.

\*\*\*

"Hey, I got one of those phones next!" James declared to the four guys occupying the four phones.

He'd just returned from intake, where he was re-booked on an aggravated assault charge. He was livid, although the allegations were true. The incident occurred back in December – six months ago – but, James remembered it like it was yesterday.

He and the crew had ventured to The Ritz, on the weekend before Christmas. Inside the club, he and Fred were seated, conversing with two females, while Ray and Black were out on the floor with the crowd. While enjoying the company of the women, James and Fred did their best to keep Ray and Black in their line of visions, being that the club, as well as the dance floor, was full. So, it was difficult, they were in and out of view. At one time, when they were both out of view, a fight had ignited on the floor.

James and Fred were out of their seats in no time, pushing through the crowd to where the main event was. That's when they saw that Ray and Black were part of the altercation, going blow-for-blow with some dudes. At the same time, they'd showed up, a few other dudes clearly comrades of the rivals, since they were all sporting black bandannas around their heads and necks- had also shown up to assist their friends. That made it four against five, until security stepped in, applying their tactics to gain control.

While the rivals got aggressive with the three bouncers. Fred took that opportunity and gestured for his crew to make a quick exit. They all knew what was up, so when they made it to Fred's car, everybody grabbed their guns. Fred gave Ray the keys and insisted that he drive to the edge of the parking lot and wait. Ray did, but by the time he'd made it to the edge, the group was exiting the club.

As if the plot was synchronized, Black, James, and Fred stepped out from where Fred's car had been parked and opened fire on them at a distance of about sixty yards. The line outside the club, dispersed as people ran for their lives. The gang attempted to flee but were forced to the ground by the barrage of slugs.

The news had reported that all of them were injured, but three of them were in critical condition. James didn't know how many he'd hit, until today. The ballistic study showed that he'd assaulted one of them. He didn't deem the results were accurate, which was a good thing, because he knew he'd hit at least three of them. The only thing he regretted now was that he didn't dispose of the gun.

Now, one of the men had concluded his call and was looking around searching for whoever was next. James didn't wait to see who it was. He snatched the receiver from the guy's hand and intentionally bumped into him for added measure. James stared him down, but the man was wise.

"Bruh, I'm not trying to fight you 'bout these folks shit," he said.

"I hope not!" James spat with raised eyebrows.

"Yo, I had that phone next, homeboy!" someone shouted.

James looked up to see who the voice belonged to. He was slowly descending the stairs.

The leader! James maintained steady eye contact until he was standing several feet away from him. He didn't have to look around for the followers because out of the corners of his eyes, he could see that they'd all stopped what they were doing and were now watching. James also noticed that Boss had emerged from his cell and was making his way towards them.

"You heard what I said?" the guy asked.

"Yeah," James answered. "You said something about having the phone next."

"That's exactly what I said!"

"I thought so." James looked over at Boss, who was standing off to his side, then back at his opponent. "If you want it, take it!"

The man's head snapped back like the words had physically struck him. He looked around for his crew, but they were as stupefied as he was. Clearly, they were not accustomed to such an adverse opponent.

James didn't have his shank on him, but at this time, he didn't feel like he needed it. Besides, he knew Boss was carrying at least two on him. Without waiting another second to see if the wanna-be-goons would advance on him, James turned his back on them and dialed the new house number he'd memorized overnight. To his surprise, there was no answer. He'd never known Kim to leave the house before ten in the morning.

After looking over his shoulder to see that everybody, including Boss, was maintaining their spot, he redialed the number, only to get the same results. This added fuel to the fire. Now, he turned on his rivals, feeling like David, ready to slay his tens of thousands of

Philistines, but almost as if on cue, somebody yelled, 'boxes on deck!'

This caused everyone to look towards the door to see that the commissary personnel had arrived. That broke the crowd up as guys went to their cells to retrieve their pillow cases to convey their store goods in. James and Boss held their positions.

"You aight, my nigga?" Boss asked.

James shook his head. "These folks just hit me with a new charge."

"Aggravated assault."

Playa Ray

# CHAPTER 17

It was 4:11 p.m. and Ray had been back and forth from Bland Town to Knight Park since eleven, trying to get off the rest of his product, so he could make a proper re-up this weekend. In Knight Park, it was just him, being that Fred was in Edgewood. In Bland Town, it was him, Twon and Big O'. As always, Big O' and Twon had purchased the rest of his weed. After selling the rest of his cocaine, Ray ventured to Northside Drive and got something to eat at Burger King. After leaving there, he re-entered Bland Town and parked at his mother's house. The master lock on the screen door showed that she wasn't home, so he sat on the trunk of his car, enjoying his meal.

Moments after Ray finished his food and discarded the trash, a flat-bed wrecker pulled up, parking across the street. Ray couldn't help but smile back at the face smiling at him from the passenger's side.

"Hey, my son!" his mother beamed.

"I see you done finally got out the house," he said.

"Yeah, Robert wanted me to spend the day with him."

By that time, Robert had circled the truck and opened the door, helping her down. Ray kissed his mother on the cheek and shook Robert's hand.

"How ya' doin', Ray?" Robert asked.

"I'm decent," Ray answered. "You?"

"I can't complain, I live it one day at a time."

"That's the move."

"Has James called you?" asked Mary.

"No."

"I wonder why he hasn't called anybody," she said. "You don't think he got in trouble, do you?"

"I hope not," Ray answered. "But I'll find out tomorrow."

"You told him I'll be up there Saturday?"

"Yeah."

"And how's Kim?" she inquired. "Have you checked on her?"

Ray was not in the mood to talk about Kim. He still hadn't figured out what to do about the situation. He was still wondering if he should spy on her. The more he thought about doing it, the more unnecessary the task seemed, being that he had a bigger task to complete.

"She's good," Ray answered. "Maybe you should call and check on her."

\*\*\*

If Fred wasn't serious about his new plan, he would've detoured a long time ago. Now, he pulled up in Kirkwood with the intent to find Lil' Al and lay everything out to him, hoping he would accept. If not, he was going to have to enlist Ray, or forfeit, and forfeiting wasn't an option.

As he cruised through the apartment, he spotted Lil' Al's gray Ford Expedition and parked beside it. As he got out, he saw Lil' Al storming in his direction with the face of fury.

"Say, Lil' Al," Fred spoke as Lil' Al approached his truck, disarming the alarm.

"What's up, shawty?" he muttered, regarding Fred with a mere glance, then opening the driver's door preparing to mount.

"You got a minute?"

"Now's not the time my man," Lil' Al stated, slowly shaking his head. "This bitch done called me with some bullshit 'bout my kids! I'll murk something 'bout my babies, my nigga!"

Fred could only nod. He didn't have kids, but he could imagine the things he would do for them if he had some. Looking over the top of his car at Lil' Al, made Fred think about the baby mama drama the everyday man went through, no matter how good of a father they were to their children. The same drama Fred was not yet ready for.

"You gotta catch me some other time," Lil' Al stated.

"I'll do that," Fred told him, then watched as he raced out of the parking lot.

\*\*\*

Black did not want to believe he was dialing the right number. After the operator had informed him – for the fifth time – that the number had been disconnected. Black placed his cell phone on Connie's coffee table and picked up his cup of Paul Masson, downing the rest of it.

After he'd gotten off the phone with Nikki, earlier, Black had uncontrollably broken down and cried. He felt like his whole world had just crumbled in front of him, but he knew, it was all his fault. After hours of sulking and cursing himself for his stupidity, Black regained his composure, showered, then caught a cab back to Connie's place with the gift basket he'd bought for Nikki.

He offered it to Connie, but she wouldn't accept it, being that it was intended for another woman. Now, he, Connie, Meeka, and Sylvia were assembled in Connie's living room, enjoying weed and a bottle of Paul Masson. Black didn't know if he was tripping or not, but he could have sworn Sylvia – who was seated across from him – kept cutting her eyes at him.

He'd also noticed that she didn't pour herself a drink, nor hit the blunts when they were passed around. All she did was operate the stereo and conduced to the conversation the women were having. Not once had she mentioned Ray. There was something strange about the way she was acting and not acting but Black was too consumed with alcohol to know if he was accurately perceiving the scene from a proper perspective.

While the women were still chatting about getting jobs and degrees, Black felt the liquor running through him. As fast as the alcohol would permit him to move, he got up and staggered towards the bathroom.

Sylvia watched as Black disappeared into the bathroom, then made the move she'd been anticipating all day. She grabbed Black's phone off the table – disregarding the looks her friends were giving her – and dialed Ray's number.

\*\*\*

It was well after eight when Ray entered his home. Enroute, he'd placed calls to Fred and Black but was only able to contact Fred. Therefore, he left a message for Black to call him back. After eating and showering, Ray wasn't at all tired, so, he grabbed his remote, laid across the bed, and surfed the channels until he came across one of his favorite sitcoms, *'Sanford and Son.'*

"That boy Fred G. Sanford!" Ray said aloud, tossing the remote and propping his head up on a pillow.

Moments later, while Ray was well into the next episode of *Sanford and Son*, his cell phone vibrated on the stand. He grabbed it and quickly answered, seeing that it was Black's number on the screen.

"It's about time!" Ray asserted.

"Ain't it?" the female's voice took him by surprise.

Ray didn't need to hear another word to know who the voice belonged to. How the hell did Black let her trick him out of his phone when Ray had already put him on point about the situation.

"Where's Black?" Ray asked, not in the mood for whatever games she intended to play with him.

"In the bathroom," she replied, then, as if she could see the inquisitive look on Ray's face, she explained. "We're at Connie's apartment. Black went to the bathroom and left his phone on the table. Need I say more?"

"What'd you want?" Ray asked, ready to get it over with.

"We need to talk."

"I'm listening."

"Face-to-face."

"It can't be said over the phone?"

"Anything can be asserted over the phone," Sylvia told him. "But what I need to say to you has to be done face-to-face."

Ray didn't know what to make of this, but he could sense the urgency in her voice. He wanted to get this over with, so he knew he had to agree to a tryst.

"Where?" he asked.

"Where are you?"

"At home."

"You don't mind driving over here?"

"How else am I supposed to get there?" he asked, not meaning to sound sarcastic. "I'll call you when I reach Chapel Road."

"Hold on," she said, then spoke to someone in the background. To Ray, she said, "Connie said I can use her car. I'll meet you in the Flea Market's parking lot. That okay with you?"

"That'll work."

After concluding the call, Ray re-dressed and made his exit. Sylvia was already there, sitting on the hood of Connie's car when he arrived. The store was closed for the night, so the Ford was the only car in the vast parking lot. Ray parked beside it, walked around to the right side of his car and leaned against the fender, facing Sylvia, who was wearing a light-colored sundress and stilettos.

Her hair, accommodated with weave, was combed back into a ponytail that graced her shoulders. The bang that almost covered her left eye, seemed to add a few years to her face. He was surprised to see that she was sitting with her legs crossed, like a lady! Being that Ray was accustomed to the things, women did to get what they want, he regarded her display as a ploy to reel him back into her life.

"So, how are you?" she asked, sounding formal.

"I'm decent," he answered. "How 'bout you?"

"I'm fine," she cleared her throat. "Can I ask you something?"

"I'm listening."

"Did I do anything wrong?"

"What'd you mean?"

"For you to leave me like that," she replied. "I mean, when I first met you, I sensed you were different from most men."

"I am different from most men."

"So, why was I jilted?"

"Is this why you called me out here?"

"No," she said. "But I feel, I deserve to know why I was thrown aside like yesterday's trash."

"Is that how you look at it?"

"How else am I supposed to look at it?" she asked, keeping her voice calm. "I thought we had something special."

"I told you, in the beginning, I didn't want a relationship."

Sylvia looked like she was considering this, then said, "Yeah, you're right, you did say that."

"So, what's the real reason you called me out here?" Ray asked, looking at his arm where his watch would've been, had he not forgotten to put it on.

"Well—" she started, "—I was trying to figure out how to tell you, but I guess I'll just flat-out tell you, I'm pregnant."

Ray was silent, perhaps stunned. Or was he mad? To be honest, Ray didn't know how he felt at this moment as he studied Sylvia. He'd always wanted a baby, but he wanted to be financially stable before bringing a child into this world. Then, as if God was using it as a sign, he thought back to when Trina tried to put another man's baby off on him.

His thoughts were interrupted, when Sylvia slid off the hood of the car and opened the driver's door, attempting to depart.

"What're you doing?" Ray asked, with a tone he didn't recognize.

Sylvia stopped, regarding him with tears in her eyes. "I'ma have my baby, no matter what!" she promised. "If you don't wanna be a man and take care of your responsibility, that's on you! I'm not gonna chase you, or force it on you." Now, tears were rolling down her cheeks.

"Man hold the hell up!" Ray took offense, approaching her, so their faces were within inches of each other. "Don't talk down on me like I'm less than the man I've worked so hard to become! You don't know me like that!

"Ray, I don't wanna raise this child alone," she said. "But I will if I have to."

"If the child is mine, you don't have to," he assured her.

"If?"

"You wouldn't object to a paternity test, would you?"

"No," she answered. "You have every right to take one."

"I'ma let you know now," he started. "If you take me on the *Maury Show*, I'm going to jail!"

"Why'd you say that?" she asked, wiping tears from her eyes.

"Cause I'ma kick your ass on national T.V.!" he teased. "The crowd will be screaming, Jerry! Jerry!"

That made her laugh and wrap her arms around his waist as Ray kissed her passionately.

***

"And you're just gonna go along with that shit?" James asked Ray, studying him through the small holes of the visitation booth.

He couldn't believe his brother, being the true misogynist that he was let some maggot-ass slut trick him into having unprotected sex with her, and not only was the bitch claiming to be pregnant, but Ray appeared to be ecstatic about it. This was not the same Ray he'd known all his life!

"I'ma go about it the right way," Ray told him. "I'll stick around until the baby's born. If the test proves it's mine I'll make sure to be the dad you and I never had. I'm sure you'll do the same."

"I respect your decision," James said. "But Kim's baby is not mine. I know this."

"How?" Ray asked, still unable to believe Kim would let another man impregnate her. He'd already validated she was lying.

"Cause I didn't get none of the symptoms men get when they get a bitch pregnant," James answered.

Ray leaned forward, "What symptoms?"

"You might wake up feeling nauseous," James said. "That's the common symptom. Some niggas might throw up a few times. It don't last that long."

"Who told you that?" Ray asked, hoping James was making all of this up.

"I'm speaking from experience," James told him. "But we'll talk about that some other time."

James was not ready to talk about the rendezvous that almost made him a father a few years ago. He was more than happy when he learned that she wasn't ready for maternity. So, they went half on an abortion.

"Well, I had those symptoms," Ray admitted.

"Should I congratulate you now?"

Ray simpered, "Very funny. Now, can we get down to business?"

"Business?"

"Unless you plan on staying in here."

"Let's talk!" said James, becoming serious at the mentioning of his freedom.

"You got over three stacks in your stash, right?"

"Yeah."

"I got over five," Ray told him. "I haven't gotten up with the crew about theirs yet, but I'ma get at them about pitching in to cop you a cheap lawyer."

"A cheap lawyer?"

"A cheap lawyer is better than a public pretender," Ray proclaimed.

"Yeah. I can't argue with that. They didn't find the shit on me, so the case shouldn't be too hard to beat."

"I hope not."

# CHAPTER 18

"Man, y'all walk like some great-grand mamas!" Ray told Kim and Sylvia, who were both now four months pregnant.

They were moving along the corridors of Grady Memorial Hospital, where Kim and Sylvia managed to get their monthly checkups scheduled for the same dates.

These past three months had been quite uphill for Ray, but he'd accomplished and maintained a great deal in that period. He'd gotten with Fred and Black and managed to hire James a lawyer for twelve thousand dollars to handle all charges, including the assault charge. Still not interested in taking a plea, the attorney filed a motion for a speedy trial. Now they were waiting for the motion to be heard.

Ray had also been able to step up his product. Now, he was selling ounces and twenty-dollar bags of weed. Being that there were no other weed men in 1020, his apartment – before he'd realized it – had become the weed spot. This was good because his customers didn't only consist of Bolton Road. There were people from Bankhead Courts, Dogwood, Bowen Homes, and other parts on and off Bankhead Highway that came through to shop with him.

Ray didn't intend to trap out of the place he rested his head, but the money was looking too good to stop now. On an average day, he would collect around six hundred dollars, which provided him with his, as well as Kim's and Sylvia's affairs. Every check he got from working at Kroger's on Howell Mill Road, went into the account he'd opened two months ago.

"It's your fault!" Sylvia shot over her shoulder at Ray, who was walking behind them.

"Girl speak for yourself!" Kim said jabbing Sylvia with her elbow.

"I am!" Sylvia returned the jab with her own elbow.

Ray just shook his head at the two women who'd become best friends since day one. When they got to the exit, the double doors automatically slid open, inviting them out into the August heat that was gradually decreasing as the month grew shorter. Ray couldn't wait for next month, so he could prove that Sylvia was having a girl like he was hoping for, and not a boy, which she was hoping for.

"Baby, can we go to McDonald's?" Sylvia asked, wrapping her arm around Ray's waist. "I want one of those grilled chicken salads."

"Yeah, I want one too," Kim agreed like a small child.

"Children—children!" Ray said, throwing his arms over their shoulders. "Must thou be so spoiled?"

They all laughed, nearing the car, where Ray opened the door for them both. After making the trip to McDonald's, Ray dropped Kim off at home to get ready for work. Patrice would pick her up later.

"Are you coming back after you get your hair braided?" Sylvia asked on the drive to Overlook, Atlanta, where she still stayed with her aunt.

"I should," he replied.

"If Tasha don't wear you out, huh?"

Ray said nothing. He was not going through this with her again. Every time it was time for him to get his hair braided, Sylvia went into a jealous frenzy, accusing him of Tasha, saying he was probably paying her in sex, in lieu of money. There were a few times when she'd demanded that he take her with him, and each time, Ray refused to defer her inconclusive assumptions.

"It would be nice to get some dick before my aunt gets home from work," she stated, breaking the silence once they'd pulled into the entrance of her apartments. "Don't make me beg! You know I will."

"It won't do you no good," he told her. "I already didn't have time to take my hair down."

"I'll take it down for you," she insisted. "I can't braid, but I can unbraid."

All Ray could do was smile at his girlfriend's persistence as he pulled up to the stairs that led up to her apartment.

"Two minutes," she said, giving him that look she always gave him when she wanted something."

"Baby, you'll have to put that thing on ice until I get back," he told her, putting his hand between her legs, caressing her womanhood through the fabric of her capri pants.

She parted her legs wider, inviting the only sensation she was going to get from him at this time. "Baby, this isn't helping," she said, already feeling the wetness seep through her panties.

Before she could close her eyes and relish this feeling, the sounds of a stereo system vibrating the car, diverted her attention. She turned in her seat, and Ray observed the SUV through the rearview mirror. The truck, a white Chevy Tahoe with matching rims, rode past the driver's side of the Delta and parked in a respectable slot of the parking lot, with the rear facing them. Ray was too busy admiring the truck to see the apprehension written all over Sylvia's face.

"Ray!" she punched him in the arm. "I gotta pee, gimme kiss."

Ray leaned in and accepted the briefest kiss she'd ever bestowed upon him.

"Hurry up and make it back!" she told him, "and be careful!"

"No doubt."

"Love you."

Love you, too."

Taking her pocketbook and McDonald's bag in tow, she was out of the car and racing up the stairs. He watched as she fussed with her keys. Once she'd got the door open, she cast one last glance at the Delta, then at the SUV before rushing inside.

*** 

Daddy watch this!" Nicole said, before turning a cartwheel and landing on her knees in the grass. She was a few feet away from where Nikki was seated on a bench beside Black, who was holding Lil' Keith.

This was the first time he'd seen them since Nikki eluded their so-called abusive relationship. They were staying with Nikki's parents until Nikki met some guy, who they were now staying with. Black was highly opposed to her decision, not willing to trust another man around his kids, but there was nothing he could do about it. Well at least, not now.

"You're supposed to land on your feet baby girl," Black told his daughter, who was the spitting image of her mother.

"I know," she stood brushing the dirt off her knees. "Uncle Willie said I have to practice, to be perfect."

"Uncle?" Black said with disgust, beaming at Nikki.

"I don't see nothing wrong with her calling him *'uncle'*," she replied.

"You don't?"

"She knows who her daddy is!" There was much attitude in her voice.

"Daddy!" Nicole intervened before Black could retort. "Mommy said I'ma start school this year."

"I know," Black now regarded his daughter. "Are you ready?"

"Yes."

It was Thursday, and Nikki was taking the kids back to Florida tomorrow night. Therefore, Black decided to curb his reprimands and enjoy the time he was bided to spend with them. What he really wanted to do was find out what hotel they were staying at, drive out there, and confront *'Uncle Willie'*, who was there now awaiting their return, but he knew he had to handle the situation more wisely if he wanted to get back on Nikki's good side.

***

"Fred, I'm not gonna kill, my baby!" Tee bristled. "Ain't no way in hell!"

"We're not prepared for a child, Tee," Fred said, looking over at Tee, who was seated in the passenger seat, looking out the side window avoiding his gaze.

They were sitting in the driveway of her parent's house on Tilson Road. Once they found out Tee was pregnant, they coaxed her into moving in with them, being that she was their only child and was having their first grandchild.

"Trust me," Tee said, now glaring at him. "If you won't help me with our baby, my parents will, but I'm not killing my baby! You can forget that!" She got out, slammed the door and stormed off towards the house.

Fred wasn't in the mood to play Romeo and Juliet, so he backed out of the driveway and rolled out, with no destination in mind. But that was how these past few months has had him – with no destination. As he drove, he thought about the bank robbery Lil' Al and Dre pulled off with another man, who was found dead the next morning, still sporting the attire, a ski mask and the gun used in the robbery.

Plus, the news claimed that a gun found on the body, was the one used to shoot the bank officer in the knee, but they didn't have to assert who they thought had liquidated the man, because it was evident. Dre and Al hadn't been back to Kirkwood, or Edgewood. Perhaps they'd found out that the guy they'd killed was the cousin of a Drop Squad affiliate.

***

"How did everything go, baby?" Connie asked when she entered her apartment clad in her work uniform, where she did housekeeping at the Mark Inn with Sylvia and her aunt.

"Everything was aight," Black answered dryly. He was sitting on the sofa, watching T.V., and did not regard her when he spoke.

"How are the babies?"

"They cool."

Connie placed her purse on the table and sat down beside him, holding his hand in hers. "Just maintain, baby. She controls the options, right now. Play by her rules until they change."

Black finally made eye contact with Connie, who'd been overly-supportive since his break-up with Nikki. She'd even insisted that he move in with her, to elude the memories that haunted him at his apartment in Capital Homes. Black took her up on her offer, but maintained the rent, in hopes of Nikki's return.

"She took my kids," Black stated.

"No, she did not," Connie assured. "She's doing what she thinks is best."

There was a knock at the front door.

"That's for you," Connie said, retrieving her purse, heading for the bedroom. "I'll start dinner after I shower."

Black answered the door. It was one of his customers wanting to purchase a hit of cocaine. He had taken Fred's advice and opened up shop in Connie's spot. The money didn't come as fast as it did in Capital Homes, but he didn't have to stand outside in the hot sun to make it.

\*\*\*

"I'm glad you're here!" Fred's mother exclaimed as soon as he'd entered the house. "I'm hungry, but I'm scared to go to the kitchen and fix me something."

"Scared of what?"

"There's a dead rat on the floor!" she stated, eyes the size of half-dollars. "And don't go telling me how dead rats can't hurt no-body!"

"I've never seen it happen," Fred joked, smiling at his mother, who resembled a frightened child in her favorite recliner.

"Very funny!" she smiled back.

"Jay Leno, huh?"

"Yeah. I'ma see if I can get you a spot on the show."

Enjoying this laugh with his mother, eased some of the tension Fred had been accumulating the past few months. After he discarded the demised rodent, he was hands and then helped his mother prepare a meal, in which they enjoyed together in the living room and reminisced on the old days.

"I'll get the dishes." Fred insisted when his mother yawned for the second time.

Before she could respond, he grabbed his plate off the coffee table, hers off her lap, then made for the kitchen. His mother had already retreated to her room by the time he finished. So, he cut off the T.V. in the living room and retired to his own. Using his key, he unlocked his closet and stood back, admiring his gun collection. The four guns he'd purchased for the robbery were still in the same place since the day he'd shown them to his fellas.

As he thought of that, he couldn't help but think of Dre and Lil' Al. Fred just knew the lick was going to take place, once he'd recruited them, but after hearing about the bank heist, he'd once again, lost hope. He couldn't even remember the last time he'd driven by the house to case it out.

\*\*\*

"What if you find out the baby's not yours?"

Ray shot a skeptical look out the driver's window at Tasha, who was standing beside the car. She expected to get laid after braiding his hair but was highly disappointed when he told her he had to get back to Sylvia, immediately, and perform sexual healing on her. That's when Tasha started making cutting remarks about Sylvia. Not once had she mentioned the baby, until now, which caused Ray to take offense.

"What kind of question is that?" he asked.

"It may not be yours."

"That's not for you to consider, Tasha!"

"Ray, I care about you," she admitted. "And I honestly hope the baby is yours. I really do, it's just that—"

Ray watched her, expecting her to finish. Instead, she turned and hurried back to her apartment, slamming the door behind her. He saw the tears welling in her eyes before she rushed off. He wanted to console her, but right now, he was tired and not in the mood to play *Dr. Phil*. So, he pulled off, making a mental note to call and check on her later.

Ray entered Overlook Atlanta and parked beside the white Chevy Tahoe that was still in the same spot. He armed his alarm, then ascended the stairs to Sylvia's apartment and knocked on the door. He thought he'd seen the curtains in the living room move, but there was no answer. He knocked again.

"I'm coming! I'm coming!" Sylvia sounded afar off.

Seconds later, she opened the door, clad in her nightgown and house shoes, with her hair wrapped in a scarf as if she was ready for bed. "Come on in, boo."

Ray entered, but to his surprise, there was another man sitting on the living room sofa.

"This is my cousin, Corey," she spoke quickly as if reading Ray's inquisitive expression. "Corey, this is my man, Ray."

"What up homie!" Corey stood, giving Ray dap.

"I can't call it," Ray replied.

Corey turned to Sylvia. "I gotta bounce. Hit me up if you need something."

"Okay."

He hugged her, then left and Sylvia locked the door.

"Where's your aunt?" Ray asked.

"In her room, like always," she answered. "I think she has company."

"You heard her moaning?" he asked, with a raised eyebrow and a smirk on his face.

She giggled. "Shut up, fool!"

"So, you heard *him* moaning?" That sounded more like a statement than a question.

Sylvia could not suppress her laughter, but Ray's attention was seized by the sound of loud music coming from outside. He peered through the curtains and saw that the music was coming from the Chevy Tahoe as it was pulling off.

"That's your cousin's truck?" he asked facing Sylvia.

"Th—the white one?" she stuttered.

"Yeah."

"Yeah, that's his," she answered. "Why?"

Dude got some major quad in there!" Ray commended. "He'll be deaf in a few years!"

She laughed nervously. "Don't say that!"

"I'm joking," he said, moving closer and wrapping his arms about her waist. "I guess I didn't make it back in time, huh?"

"I told you to give me some before she got here."

This was not working for Ray. Now he was in need of sexual healing, but ever since Sylvia's aunt claimed to have heard them going at it, they'd been sneaking around like a couple of teenagers, and Ray remembered that day well.

*That was the day Sylvia begged him to perform anal sex on her. At first, Ray declined, but the Queen of Seduction would not let up, so as always, he gave in. She taught him how to lubricate her first, then loosen her up with his fingers, one at a time. When the time came for him to enter her, she cautioned him to insert the head of his penis, and slowly work the rest, but once he felt the tightness of her hole wrap around his rod, something took control, prompting him to ram every inch of his manhood inside of her.*

*She moaned in protest, which only added fuel to the fire. Ray gripped her waist and pounded with consistency. Apparently, Sylvia had forgotten that her aunt was home, because she screamed at the top of her lungs, begging him to stop, but he didn't stop until he exploded inside of her.*

"You wanna slide to my crib real quick?" he now asked.

"I would love to," she said. "But I'm tired, plus, I have to go to work in the morning."

"Yeah, me too," he gave in. "I guess I'll see you tomorrow."

"Okay baby."

They kissed, and Ray was out the door, feeling like he'd been rejected. He had to accept the fact that Sylvia was tired because they'd been at the hospital all morning. To be honest, Ray was feeling a bit fatigued himself, but it was only a few minutes after seven and he did not plan on turning in this early. He could visit James, but he and his mother had already made plans to visit him Saturday, with a special surprise visit from their sister, April, who was scheduled to arrive tomorrow.

On his drive home, Ray could not stop thinking about the way Tasha behaved. He could understand that she was jealous of what he had with Sylvia, which was noticeable, but to include the child was beyond reproach, and he was going to get on her about that when he called her tonight.

As he pulled into Maple Creek Apartments, Ray saw a car parked in the spot he usually parks in. The car, a black four-door Chevy Caprice on chrome wheels, belonged to Snap from Bankhead Courts. Ray was curious because he'd never known Snap to hang out at 1020. The only time he'd come through was to buy weed from Ray.

He pulled alongside the Chevy. The windows were down, and Snap was accompanied by three women. "What up, Playa-Playa!" Snap greeted, smiling.

"I can't call it, Slick Pimpin'," Ray answered. "What the move is?"

"Boy, I need somma that get right!" Snap told him. "I done drove from hood to hood, city to city and planet to planet. Niggas are out!"

"You mean to tell me them niggas on Mars ain't got none?" Ray laughed.

"Man, them niggas are out, too!"

They all burst into laughter including the women.

"Well, let me park," Ray told him.

By the time he parked, Snap was already standing by his apartment door. They entered, and Ray retrieved the scale, weighed up an ounce for Snap, then threw in an extra twenty sack.

"Boy, you do good business!" Snap told Ray. "That's why I fuck wit'cha!"

"Hell, I appreciate the business."

"That's what's up," they dapped. "I'll leave one of my girls with you if you want me to."

"Nah, I'm cool," Ray lied.

Snap left, Ray went to the refrigerator to see what he was going to fix himself to eat.

\*\*\*

Friday had finally rolled around, and Ray was about twenty minutes away from his lunch break. He only had thirty minutes. But for some reason, he wanted to drive out to the Mark Inn on Fulton

Industrial and engage in a quickie with Sylvia, in one of the vacant rooms like they'd done on several occasions. He could not stop thinking about her since they'd had phone sex, last night.

Ray heard men claim that pregnant pussy was the best pussy, but he figured it was just another saying from the men's mythical book of quotes. Now, he was a firm believer, because there wasn't a day that went by that he didn't long for Sylvia's always hot, always wet, pregnant pussy. Yes, he was always ready to feed the baby.

"I'm closed for lunch," Ray told a customer who approached his counter with a shopping cart full of groceries.

He had enough time to take a few customers, but right now, he was thinking with his other head.

But he had to devise a plan that would get him the rest of the day off. By the time he reached the main office with the drawer from his register, he concluded that he didn't need a plan. Being that Jessica, the shift's supervisor, had a crush on him. She'd been flirting with him since he started.

"You're mighty early," Jessica said, checking her watch. She was seated at her desk doing paperwork when he entered.

"I am?" Ray asked, well aware of her accusation.

"Twelve minutes early to be exact."

"Is that a good thing or bad thing?" Ray sat his drawer down on the desk in front of her.

"Suppose I said it was a bad thing?" she asked, surveying him with lustful eyes.

"I guess I would have to apologize."

"I don't accept apologies," she said, looking down at his crotch, then back into his eyes. "You would have to make it up to me."

Ray could not deny that Jessica, at the age of thirty-nine, was one fine woman. However, he'd heard about the last cashier she'd been lingering with. It was supposed to have been a sex thing, but Jessica went into a jealous rage when she caught him making passes at a female customer. As if grilling him in front of everybody wasn't enough, the very next day, she terminated him, claiming his drawer came up short.

Ray pitied the guy after hearing the story, but like the song says: *"It takes a fool—"*

"I also came to ask you if I could have the rest of the day off," Ray said, now wishing he'd come up with an excuse.

"For what reason?" She leaned forward, propping her elbows on the desk. "You don't look sick."

"I'm not sick," he answered, hating that she'd beat him to the punch. "I just don't feel too well."

She sighed and leaned back in her chair, eyeing him for a long period of time. "Alright." She finally gave in. "But you owe me."

"No doubt."

Ray already knew what she was intimating, but he didn't have any plans to engage in any of her lascivious fantasies. She gave him his check and he was out the door. He pulled into the Mark Inn's parking lot, parking close to the entrance. As he dismounted and made it for the front office, he noticed Sylvia's cousins truck parked farther down, with the rear facing him. The lights indicated that the vehicle was activated.

Ray entered the office and approached the desk, where a Black female in her mid-forties was filing her fingernails.

"Welcome to the Mark Inn!" She beamed, revealing perfectly white teeth. "How may I help you?"

"Can you page Sylvia Baker for me?"

"She's out on her break."

"How long has she been on break?" Ray was reluctant to believe that Sylvia had taken a break without calling to sexual harass him like she'd always do.

"I don't know exactly," she answered. "But it's been over twenty minutes. She should be back shortly."

"Thank you."

Ray exited the office and stood in front of the building, surveying the lot, until he spotted Sylvia's aunt's car parked a few cars away from Connie's, both unoccupied. Sylvia would usually use one of those cars when she set out to get something to eat on her break. Perhaps the receptionist was wrong. Maybe she'd gotten

Sylvia mixed up with someone else because Sylvia would never break without calling him, and vice versa.

That's when he focused his attention on the Chevy Tahoe that sat at the far end of the lot, still running. Apparently, her cousin had taken her out for lunch. Ray would have waited until she got out of the truck, but he didn't come out here to wait. Therefore, he set his feet in motion and headed for the truck. Since the windows were factory-tinted, Ray couldn't tell if anyone was inside, but as he got within five yards of the vehicle, he noticed that Corey was the only occupant.

Ray's thought was to detour, but his feet kept moving as if they were drawn by some magnetic force. They didn't stop until he reached the driver's door, where the window was rolled down a few inches. What he saw made him feel like an intruder. Corey was reclined in his seat, biting on his bottom lip, with his eyes closed, while receiving oral sex from the female passenger. As if sensing Ray's presence the second he approached, Corey opened his eyes, but his expression quickly went from alarmed to apprehensive.

"Damn, my bad!" Ray apologized, but as he was about to turn and walk away, the female lifted her head, wiping her mouth with the back of her hand.

Her appearance was neither alarmed, nor apprehensive, but her cold and passive eyes locked with his, causing his body to freeze up. Ray brought his fist up to his mouth as if to parry the bile that rose up in his throat. His heart felt like an invisible hand was wrapped around it and was slowly increasing its grip. It seemed like the world had stopped moving. He couldn't believe he'd caught Sylvia performing the sexual act that he thought was meant for him, on another man.

Not only had she lied about Corey being her cousin – if that was his real name – she had the audacity to sit there, regarding him as if nothing was wrong. There couldn't possibly be a word to describe Ray's anger, but his facial expression must've been very obvious because their eyes simultaneously enlarged.

Then, he realized it wasn't his facial expression, but his left hand had, somehow, reached his waistband, where he kept his gun whenever he didn't wear his holster.

## CHAPTER 19

"Your Honor, my client pleads not guilty to all counts," Attorney Paul Scott stated, standing at the defense table beside James, who was still seated, clad in his jail attire.

The nineteenth of September had finally arrived, and James was ready for whatever happens. He'd managed to keep the knowledge of his court date from his mother, who would have undoubtedly told Kim. As far as he knew, only Ray, Fred, and Black were aware of his highly anticipated day and had planned to attend the preceding, but only Ray and Black showed.

James glanced back at his two-man support team for the sixth time. Although Ray seemed placid to the naked eye, James could still tell he was still hurt about catching Sylvia sucking another man's dick.

"Right now," Paul continued. "We're requesting that a reasonable bond be set for the defendant."

"Any objections from the State?" asked the Judge.

"Yes, Your Honor." The Assistant District Attorney stood. "Considering this is not the defendant's first drug charge, nor felony, the State is indisposed to counsel's request. The defendant should remain in custody until a trial date is set."

"Your Honor," Paul persisted. "I can't deny the State's assertion of the defendant's prior bad acts but allow me to tell the court that the drugs and weapon found in said case, did not belong to the defendant."

The Judge asked, "Do you have any proof of that?"

"It's in the police report, Your Honor."

"What's in the police report?"

"I don't have the exact diction of the report," Paul said. "But it claims that the contents were *not* found on the accused."

"Your Honor," the D.A. intervened. "That report is unimportant at the time."

"If that is so," said the Judge. "Then all charges should be dismissed at this time. Now, does the report matter or not?"

"Yes, Your Honor," the D.A. deferred.

"Does the report corroborate the counsel's claim?"

"Yes, Your Honor."

"So, the items were not found on the defendant's person?"

"No, Your Honor."

\*\*\*

Fred looked at his watch, he'd been sitting in the waiting area of the abortion clinic for over two hours. Tee had been called to the back, over forty-five minutes ago. He should have been at James' preceding, but Tee informed him last night that her appointment was today. He knew he had to accompany her because that was part of the deal, but he was not going to give her the twenty-five hundred dollars until after the procedure.

While he was mulling over how long this may take, his cell phone vibrated inside his pants pocket. He retrieved it to see Ray's number on the screen.

"What's the word?" he answered.

"A hundred thousand," Ray told him.

"For everything?"

"Yep."

"So, we need ten stacks," said Fred. "How much are you sittin' on?"

"I still got thirty-five hundred put up," Ray answered. "Black got fifteen."

"Who else pitchin' in?"

"Big O and Twon."

"What they got?"

"I haven't hit them up yet."

"Well, go ahead and hit them up," Fred told him. "Hit me back around eight."

Fred ended the call and tried to recall how much he had in his stash. He didn't bother to keep up with the amount, because it seemed like every time he turned around, he was conducting a withdrawal, taking out more than he was putting in. But it didn't matter how much he had stashed away, he would put it all up to free his comrade.

\*\*\*

"What'd he say?" Black asked when Ray got off the phone with Fred.

They were seated across from each other at the same Burger King where Kim was employed, which is where they'd decided to have lunch after leaving the courthouse.

"He told me to hit him back around eight," Ray answered.

"James' lucky he's my folk," Black said, pointing a french fry at Ray. "Cause that lil' fifteen hundred is gonna put a dent in a nigga's pocket."

"Shit, we're all looking at a dent in our pockets," Ray told him. "At the same time, we're doing it by choice."

"Nah," Black rectified. "We're doing it out of love. That's my nigga, I'll do the same for you and Fred."

"Man don't be gettin' all emotional on me 'n shit!" Ray joked.

Black laughed. "Go to hell!"

Once they'd consumed their lunch. They exited the restaurant and approached their cars that were parked side by side. Black deactivated the alarm on his dark green four-door Nissan Maxima he'd leased.

"What you 'bout to get into?" Black asked Ray.

"I'ma see what the move is with Big O' and Twon," Ray answered. "Then I'ma head to the crib and rest up until eight."

"You want the money now?"

"Nah, just hold on to it," Ray told him. "We'll put everything together later."

They dapped before departing.

As Ray drove, his mind slowly regressed to the day he'd caught Sylvia playing another man's flute. He still didn't know what he would've done, had he not left his gun in the car. He also didn't know what he would've done, had Corey not sped out of the parking lot – with Sylvia in tow – before he'd made it to his car. That was the last he'd seen or heard from Sylvia.

He couldn't even force himself to return to work, after a whole week of crying himself to sleep. He'd never returned Jessica's calls, nor called Kroger's to let them know he wasn't coming back.

"Yeah," he now answered his vibrating phone.

"Boy, I thought you had changed the number again," Kim asserted.

"Why'd you say that?"

She giggled. "Cause, I dialed your old number by mistake again."

"Which reminds me," Ray said. "They just built a new facility for mental health pregnant women."

"Shut up!" she said through her laughter.

Ray was glad that James had gotten over his suspicion of Kim being pregnant by another man because he still couldn't bring himself to believe it.

"What's on ya mind?" he asked.

"I just called to check on you," she told him. "James hasn't called yet."

"It's just after twelve."

"But he would usually call me before twelve."

She was right. James would always call her every day before twelve. As if the calls didn't cost, but it didn't matter to Ray. He was just glad they were comporting like mature adults.

"It's not the end of the world, Kim," Ray said. "He'll call."

"Guess who had the nerve to call me last night?"

"Who?"

"Sylvia," Kim answered. "We talked for a long time, too. She told me she moved and got a new job. She didn't tell me where."

'Of course not,' Ray thought.

"She also asked me for your number," Kim continued. "I told her I couldn't give it to her, so she asked me to relay the message."

"What message?"

"That you were right."

"About what?"

"She's having a girl."

\*\*\*

"Mr. Mills?"

Fred looked up from the Rolling Stones magazine he was looking through, at the mentioning of his last name. Being that this was an abortion clinic, and only women were summoned to the back, he disregarded the old White man in the long white coat and continued scanning the magazine.

"Mr. Frederick Mills?" the doctor called again.

This time, when Fred looked up, he could've sworn the doctor was looking directly at him. "What's up?" he answered.

"Are you, Mr. Mills?"

"Yeah.'

"I would like to speak to you for a moment," said the doctor.

Fred placed the magazine on the table and approached the doctor, who stepped aside to allow him entrance.

"Second room, it's unlocked."

Fred turned the knob on the indicated door and pushed it open. That's when he realized something was wrong. Tee was sitting on the patient's table, being consoled by two female nurses as she wept. Fred looked back like he was about to detour, but the doctor, who was standing behind him, motioned for him to go on in. The doctor entered behind him and, as if on cue, the nurses filed out of the room, closing the door behind them.

The doctor sat on a cushioned stool and commenced to rummaging through some papers on his desk. Fred looked over at Tee, who was staring back at him with glossy red eyes. By the looks of her stomach, he could tell that the baby was still there.

*'I hope this bitch ain't reneged on me,'* he thought.

"I'm sorry for the delay, Mr. Mills," the doctor said, swiveling around on his stool. "Now, I would usually have someone arrested for attempting this kind of offense."

"What kind of offense?" Fred looked at Tee, then back at the doctor.

"Trying to abort a fetus that's un-abortable."

"And why is it un-abortable?"

"Ms. Harris is almost five months into her pregnancy," said the doctor. "Which means she is long over-due for an abortion."

"So, why was the appointment made if y'all knew she was over-due?"

"That's the point, Mr. Mills. She claimed to our receptionist that she was only six weeks into her pregnancy. We can only go by what we're told."

Fred didn't know much about abortion clinics and their procedures but, for some reason, he felt like Tee and this doctor was conspiring against him.

***

While driving along Sylvan Road, Black made a left onto Burns Drive and shortly approached the familiar white and yellow house. He pulled into the driveway and parked behind a red BMW convertible. As much as he hated Felicia, he had to respect the fact that she was doing well for herself. Plus, she'd managed to move her and his son out of Grady Homes.

Black made it to the front door and was about to ring the doorbell when the door swung open. Felicia stood there clad in a zebra-striped bodysuit and long black hoe boots. She stood at 6'1", was light-skin, with long blond micro-braids.

"I didn't expect you to come this damn early!" she snarled. "I just got out the bed!"

"Not dressed like that!" he indicated her get-up.

"Don't worry 'bout how the fuck I'm dressed!" she spat. "And for your information, I still sleep naked."

"I wouldn't give a damn if you slept bald-headed!" Black replied.

"Where's my son?"

She opened her mouth to say something but thought against it. Instead, she turned and stormed through and out of the living room.

Black watched her ass the whole time, remembering how soft it was and how much she enjoyed anal sex.

Those were the times.

Once she'd exited the living room, Black entered the house, closing the door. He hadn't been there in a while, but every time he came by the place always looked like Felicia had called in a decorator to redecorate, and everything was highly expensive, from the crystal chandelier to the ostrich-feathered rug. He didn't like what she did to support her and his son, but at least she wasn't laying down with men for free. They had to pay to play!

Black was about to take a seat on the white leather couch covered in plastic but thought against it. Instead, he approached the huge fish tank and looked at the assortment of fish. He immediately spotted two tropical fish he didn't remember seeing.

"Daddy, you like my fish?"

Black turned to see his three-year-old son, Kevin, approaching.

"You got some new fish?" He picked his son up, kissing him on the cheek.

"Yes," Kevin answered. "Mama bought 'em for me."

"Which ones?"

"That one and that one." Kevin pointed from one tropical fish to the other, leaving his fingerprint on the glass as he did.

"What kind of fish are they?"

"Um—" Kevin turned to his mother for assistance.

"Barracudas," she answered.

Black almost asked how much they cost, but quickly curbed that thought. To do so, would only give her room to boast and brag. Black was not in the mood to be reminded of how her pussy was accumulating more money than the crumbs he was pedaling.

Instead, he asked his son, "When is your birthday?"

"Tomorrow," he answered. "But my birthday party is on Saturday, at Auntie Becky's house. Are you coming?"

"Nah, I won't be able to make it baby," Black said. "But I did get you a birthday present."

Kevin's face lit up. "You did!"

"Of course, I did." Black smiled at his son. "But I left it in the car. You gotta go and get it."

Black put his son down, with the intention of walking him to the car, but as soon as Kevin's feet touched the carpet, he sprinted for the door and was out of it in seconds.

"I hope you didn't get him no dog!" Felicia said to Black's back as he made for the door.

"Shit, he already got one of those," he said over his shoulder, exiting.

To his surprise, she didn't respond, but when he made it to his car, where Kevin was waiting by the passenger door. He noticed her standing in the threshold, looking attentively at the car.

"That's it right there, daddy?" Kevin asked, pointing at the gift bag on the passenger seat.

"I don't know," Black answered, deactivating the alarm. "Check it out."

Kevin swung the door open and grabbed the bag off the seat. "Oohhh, my friend got one of these!" he exclaimed, pulling out the hand-held video game.

While he was marveling over his new toy, Black diverted his attention to the turquoise Monte Carlos on gold Dayton's that pulled in front of the house, quietly, except for the sounds from the dual pipes indicating the Super Sport wasn't just for looks.

The driver's door swung open and the man who emerged from the car looked to be in his late thirties.

'One of Felicia's customers?' Black thought.

"Hey, Rico!" Felicia beamed as he ascended the steps to the porch.

He hugged her and said something inaudible to Black, but whatever it was had to be pertaining to him because they both looked in his direction.

"That's Kevin's, dad," he heard her say in a low tone like she expected him not to hear.

Rico took a split second to size Black up, then entered the house, brushing Felicia in the process, but not before Black caught a glimpse of the ominous charm that hung from his Cuban link chain.

Playa Ray

# CHAPTER 20

Ray pulled into Maple Creek, pressing the power button on his radio, turning it off. As he neared his unit, he saw Precious. His next-door neighbor, standing in front of her door with some guy Ray had never seen before, but what struck him as odd, was how the guy's visage changed as he studied Ray's car, as if he recognized it from somewhere. He then said something to Precious, who said something back and tilted her head towards Ray's door as if telling him Ray stayed there.

Ray didn't know what was going on, but their motions had him on high alert. So, as he drove past them to make his routine U-turn to claim his spot in front of his door. He sagely canvassed the area for anything or anybody that looked suspicious.

As he parked, he saw that they were still gawking at him or was it his car? Was something wrong with his car? Had someone left some kind of marks on his baby? Of course not! He would have spotted that instantly. This really vexed him. Plus, the dude had been standing with his hands in his pockets the whole time. Whatever was about to go down, Ray did not plan on prolonging it.

After shutting off the engine, he eased his gun into his left pocket and got out. He didn't look directly at them, but observed them out the corner of his eyes, through his sunglasses, as he approached with his left hand in his pocket, firmly gripping his pistol and keys in his right hand.

"What's up, Ray!" the man spoke, once Ray was just a few feet away from them.

Apparently, Precious had told this stranger his name, but Ray standing just inches away from his door, just stood there watching him, waiting for whatever was going to ensue, but the man was smiling.

"I'm Steve," the stranger said. "I was on Rice Street with your brotha, James."

"Yeah?" Ray was a bit relieved, but not in the mood to converse. Especially with someone, he didn't know. He was tired, and all he wanted to do was rest until eight o'clock.

"Yeah," Steve replied. "I recognized the car. He told me you stayed out here."

"I guess you already know my cousin, Precious," he said, nodding in her direction.

"Yeah," Ray nodded at her, she did likewise.

"So, what's the word on, James?"

"They gave him a bond," Ray answered. "We should have that paid by tonight."

"That's what's up. I wish I could pitch in, but I'm in a bind, right now."

"It's all good," Ray told him. "I appreciate the thought. I'll let James know you asked about him."

"He got my info," Steve asserted. "Tell him to hit me up. I'm still down with the movement."

"A'ight." Ray entered his apartment, happy for the conclusion of that encounter. However, he wondered what the hell he meant when he said he was still down with the movement— what movement?

Ray was too tired to agonize on that. After placing his gun, keys, money and cell phone on the dresser. He kicked off his shoes and lied across the bed, he didn't have time to make up this morning for having to rush out to James' hearing.

It was only a matter of seconds before Ray felt his eyelids getting heavy, but as soon as sleep began to consume him, there was a knock on the door.

*'Man, I know dude ain't knocking on my door,'* he thought, thinking it was Steve. He made no attempt to get up. Seconds, later, his cell phone vibrated atop the dresser. The first person that came to his mind was Fred. Perhaps Fred had already gotten his hands on the money he was going to conduce to James' bond.

Retrieving his phone, he answered without checking the caller I.D. "Yeah?"

"Nigga answer the door!" B.J. demanded. "I know your *Snoop Dogg*-looking-ass ain't sleep!"

Saying nothing, Ray hung up, placed the phone back on the dresser and headed for the door. When he opened the door, he saw that B.J. was accompanied by T-Roc and three girls.

"You got company?" B.J. asked.

"Nah."

"Well, you do now," B.J. pushed past Ray, followed by T-Roc and the girls.

Ray closed the door and joined them in the living room, where the women had all took a seat on the sofa. T-Roc occupied the recliner, and B.J. was looking through Ray's CD book.

"Man tell me you got some dope!" B.J. said to Ray.

"You know I do."

B.J. headed for the bedroom, followed by Ray.

"What the move is?" Ray asked once they entered the room.

"You already know," said B.J. "These girls wanna smoke, drink and fuck."

\*\*\*

"What them folks talkin' bout?" Ty, James' cellmate since Steve's release asked. He was lying on his bunk when James walked in.

"They gave me a bond," James answered. "A hundred bands."

"Your brotha's gonna pay it?"

"I don't know yet," James said, grabbing a honey bun from his shelf and taking a seat on his bunk. "I'm quite sure he and the crew gonna pay it, but it might take a minute. A week or two, maybe."

"Boss came to the door looking for you."

"He's off lockdown?"

"I think he was coming back from the dentist," Ty answered. "Officer Jones brought him to the door."

James knew Officer Jones. He was one of the officers who were down-to-earth. He pretty much let the inmates do what they wanted, as long as they weren't trying to harm him or each other. So, it was nothing for Boss to talk Jones into bringing him to the fifth floor, on their way back to the seventh, where Boss was on lockdown for stabbing his cellmate and another guy.

Well, James stabbed the latter. Boss took it upon himself to take the charge. James wouldn't allow it, but Boss insisted, saying James had a better chance of getting out than he did. Now, that James was about to get out. That would make him the only ally Boss would have on the outside.

\*\*\*

After dropping Tee off at home, Fred drove home to see how much money he had in his stash, which was a little over twelve hundred since he'd subtracted twenty-five hundred to pay Tee for going along with the abortion, which never took place, but he still gave her the money for trying.

After leaving home, Fred headed for Eric's house. He didn't like asking his brother for money, but Eric had already said he would go in on the bond if they needed him to.

"They want twelve percent," Eric told Fred, upon entering the living room, where Fred sat on the sofa, holding Eric's four-month-old daughter.

"Who want twelve?" asked Fred.

"That's what it is now," Eric responded. "It's twelve percent on all bonds. I guess Ray don't know that either, huh?"

"I guess not."

"You need to go ahead and call him, so I'll know how much to pull out the stash."

\*\*\*

"I wanna fuck you!" Half Pint, who was sitting beside Ray on the sofa, whispered in his ear.

She had been flirting with Ray ever since she'd been there, blowing in his ear, kissing on his neck and throwing her leg over his. She'd even given him lap dances, where she would grind on him until she felt him grow hard. Then, she would re-take her seat beside him and marvel at the lump in his pants until it subsided.

Ray didn't like being teased but for some reason, he was enjoying her coquettish antics. Now he was looking at Half Pint, who was smiling at him. She was dark-skin and stood around 4'9'-5'0', with short auburn red hair. She told Ray that she was nineteen-years-old, but he inquired her I.D. card, which indicated that she was eighteen-years-old. That didn't matter to him, because she was considered legal in the states.

"Fire up another blunt, T-Roc!" B.J. who was reclined on the loveseat with one of the girls told T-Roc who was sitting in the recliner with the other girl sitting in his lap.

"Yeah, y'all fire up another one," Half Pint said as she stood, pulling Ray up by his hand. "We'll be back."

Ray did not protest as she pulled him towards his bedroom. Once they entered, Half Pint closed and locked the door. She then dropped to her knees in front of him and began undoing his belt while looking up into his eyes. The look in her eyes stimulated him instantly. He was hypnotized. That was until his vibrating cell phone broke the spell.

That's when he realized he'd left it on the dresser, knowing he was supposed to keep it on him in case Fred called. Just so happened, Fred's number was showing on the screen. Ray caught his shorts before they cleared his thighs and pulled them back up.

"What you doin'?" Half Pint asked. "I know you ain't gonna—"

"Talk to me!" Ray said through the phone, rejecting Half Pint's outburst.

"We need twelve stacks," Fred told him.

"Why twelve?"

While Fred explained to Ray what Eric had explained to him. Ray glanced at Half Pint, who was sitting on the edge of the bed, pouting, with her arms folded across her chest. She reminded him of Sylvia.

"What did Twon and Big O' do for it?" Fred finally asked.

"Fifteen a piece."

"So, what're we sitting on?"

"Eight."

"Hold on," Fred spoke to someone in the background, who Ray figured to be Eric. He came back to the phone and said, "Everything's on deck. Me and Sharonda's gonna meet you at Rapid Bail. She's gonna sign the bond."

"A'ight," said Ray. "I'm on my way.

"I'm going too!" Half Pint insisted when Ray concluded his call.

"You don't even know where I'm going," Ray told her. "I could be going to hell."

"Don't matter," she said. "Just make sure you stop and get us something to eat first."

'*Another Sylvia, indeed,*' Ray thought.

***

"There's no bond showing," the older woman said to Sharonda, the mother of Eric's daughter. "When did he receive the bond?"

Sharonda looked back at Ray, who was standing close to the exit along with Half Pint, Black, and Connie, who from what Ray had observed had been intermittently glowering at Half Pint. Fred was standing at the counter with Sharonda.

"This morning," Ray answered the woman's query.

"That probably wouldn't show up in the computer until after midnight," she told them.

"Well, can I go ahead and fill out the paperwork and leave the money with you?" Sharonda asked.

"You can," the lady started. "But are you sure it's a one-hundred-thousand-dollar bond?"

"That's what the judge said," Ray rejoined. "I was there."

"Well I can't argue with what you've heard," she told Ray, handing Sharonda a clipboard containing forms.

***

It was well after midnight and James and Ty were both lying on their bunks, engaged in their usual conversation about the streets, which was routine after lights out.

"Man, I ain't know you knew that nigga," James said.

"Yeah, I know that clown," said Ty. "He's Drop Squad, now."

"Bullshit!"

"Fa'real!"

"So, he's getting to the money now?" James asked.

"Hell yeah!" Ty answered. "Before I got locked up, he came through Boat Rock in a new Lexus. He had the Drop Squad Chain on."

"That nigga was lame as hell in school."

"The lames be the ones who always prosper," Ty stated.

At that time, they heard the intercom click on. "James Young, five-seventeen, pack it up! James Young, five-seventeen, pack it up!"

"What the fuck!" James leaped out of his bunk. "This shit can't be real!"

"Shit, lil' bruh came through," Ty said, sitting up in his bunk. "They're not telling you to pack it up for nothing."

"I hope not!" James said as he thought about all the plans he'd devised since he'd been incarcerated. Now he was wondering if that lick was still any good, because, right now, he was in dire need of some cash. He didn't plan on slaving at nobody's job for a measly check. He'd been pedaling crumbs ever since he could remember. It was time to get rich or die trying, and he meant that with all his heart, but first, he had to deal with that trifling ass, Kim.

Playa Ray

# CHAPTER 21

"Ray!"

The female's voice that whispered his name, and the hand that was patting him on his chest, rose him from his sleep. He opened his eyes and found himself looking into Sylvia's face.

"Somebody's knocking on your window," she whispered again and looked towards the window that lied beyond the headboard. That's when he realized it wasn't Sylvia, but Half Pint.

He noticed that her hair which was illuminated by the light from the window was still in disarray from hours of rolling in the hay. He also noticed by looking at her small, well-rounded breasts that she was still naked. He felt himself becoming aroused as he thought about their sexcapade. The girl was a worthy opponent, but she was inexperienced when it came to oral sex.

"You heard me?" Now she regarded him with apprehension in her eyes.

"What?" Apparently, he didn't hear what she'd said, or did he hear her say something about a window?

Before Half Pint could repeat whatever, it was she'd said, there was a knock at the window that caused them both to jerk their heads in that direction. Although Ray had abruptly sat up, in the same manner, Half Pint was already sitting in. He looked over at the clock, 3:52 a.m.

Since he'd been staying in Maple Creek, no one had ever knocked on his window. Hell, no one had ever ventured to his apartment at this time of the morning either. Ray didn't feel his life was in danger, but he still pulled his .380 from under his pillow, just in case.

Seeing the gun, Half Pint shrieked and dove over the side of the bed. Ray made sure to look down before he got off the bed, in case he stepped on Half Pint, but she was under the bed. It struck him as funny, but he silently promised himself to tease her about that later.

As Ray got off the bed, he flung the sheet-like curtains aside, with his gun aimed at the man's face that was just inches away from the glass, smiling at him.

"It's a good thing I didn't try to open the window," the man said, looking at the gun. "I would've been well shot!"

"I oughta shoot you anyway!" Ray stated, smiling back at his brother.

"Then, you 'll have to buy a new window," James said. Then, he noticed the silhouette of a female's head, peeking over Ray's shoulder. "I didn't know you had company."

"Yeah." Ray looked over his shoulder at Half Pint, who still looked a bit shaken up. To James, he said, "Let me put on some clothes."

He closed the curtain, tossed the gun on the bed, and studied Half Pint, who was standing with her arms folded across her chest.

"Who is that?" she asked.

"My brotha."

"The one who was locked up?"

"I only have one brotha," he asserted, donning his boxer shorts, then grabbing his shirt off the floor.

"You ain't gotta get smart!" she snapped, snatching the shirt from him before he could put it on.

"Can I have my shirt back?"

Rejecting his question, she pulled it over her head. It stopped just above her knees. She then folded her arms back over her chest and gave him a look that pretty much let him know he was not getting his shirt back until she was ready to give it back, but Ray did not oppose with this gesture. Instead, he pulled a tank top from a drawer, put it on, then exited the room with Half Pint on his heels.

"Boy, Jack Frost ain't bullshttin' out here!" James said when Ray opened the door.

"How'd you get out here?" Ray asked.

"I caught a cab," he answered, entering, hugging his brother. Seeing Half Pint, who was standing akimbo behind Ray, he asked, "Who you got wit'cha?"

"Half Pint," she took the initiative.

"Well, I'm James," he said, giving her a quick once-over.

"I know." Her curt reply won Ray an inquisitive look from James.

174

"I'm safe," Ray told her, locking the door back. "You can go back to bed."

She looked as if she was about to protest, but instead, kissed Ray on the lips and retreated. They watched as she sauntered towards the room. Once she'd entered and closed the door, James gave Ray an approving look.

"Two thumbs up?" Ray asked.

"Definitely!"

"You want in?"

"Man, pussy might be one of the last things on my mind," James replied. "Right now, I need a fat-ass blunt."

"Shit, I'm out," Ray told him. "Plus, it's a draught. Ain't no telling when I'ma re-up again.

"Okay. Fuck the blunt, hold this." He handed Ray the book he'd been holding. "I gotta piss like a racehorse!"

James headed for the bathroom. Ray surveyed the book and saw that it was a Bible.

"What the hell!" Ray said to himself, not willing to believe that James the devil himself would even be in possession of such material. Maybe he'd been converted—yeah right!

\*\*\*

It was after one o'clock when Ray had dropped Half Pint off at her home in Hollywood Courts, and he and James had journeyed to Bland Town to visit their mother. Who was apparently working with Robert again, because her car, Robert had given her, was there, but she wasn't. Therefore, they headed for Knight Park. James knew Fred was there because he'd called earlier, and laid out his plan for tonight, which included Fred and Black. Black would meet them in Knight Park a little later.

"They done let my nigga up out that bitch!" Fred asserted when he opened the front door for them.

"Shit, thanks to y'all," James said giving him dap.

"It's all love, "Fred told him. "Y'all come on in, nobody's here but me."

Right after Fred said that he shot a quick glance at Ray, who had a half-smirk on his face.

"Nigga, ain't no rats in this muthafucka!" Fred remarked. "With your scary ass!"

Ray was laughing too hard to retort. "You got that!" Was all he could muster as he entered behind James, who was also laughing.

They followed Fred to his bedroom, both sitting on the sofa. Fred retrieved a small box from the closet and handed it to James, who opened it and pulled out a black Glock .40.

"Brand new," Fred told him.

James was looking at the gun, but he was thinking about the kick-door they were supposed to have pulled before his arrest. Fred had told him, this morning, that the house was raided by authorities, two weeks ago. Now, they were going to have to scout for another drug house, but they would have to be very careful not to run up in a spot that belonged to Drop Squad.

\*\*\*

Ray was not really in the mood to deal with Tasha and her pro-miscuous behavior, but his scalp was itching and in dire need of a shampoo bath. It's not like he couldn't do it himself, he just felt that women were more adept when it came to things like that.

"Hey!" she said when she opened the door for him. She was clad in a pink sweatsuit.

"You on your way out?" he asked.

"No," she answered. "I just got back in about twenty minutes ago. Come on in." She allowed him entrance, then locked the door back. "So, what's on your mind?" she asked, smiling from ear to ear.

"I need my hair washed bad!" he told her.

"Okay. Let me get situated, then I'll get the shampoo." She exited the living room.

Ray took a seat on the sofa. For the umpteenth time, he was trying to figure out what James, Fred, and Black could possibly be up to. He knew something was up when Black picked them up in an unfamiliar, grey Honda Civic with dark-tinted windows. Whatever they were up to, he thought, had to be something they'd devised while James was incarcerated.

***

James, who was seated in the front passenger seat of the Honda, checked his watch. It was twenty minutes after eleven. He figured this was the best time to make the call, so he grabbed his cell phone from his lap and dialed.

"Burger King!" a female's voice stated. "Donna speaking."

"Has Kim left yet?" James inquired.

"Kim leaves at ten, sir."

"Okay, thank you." James ended the call.

"What'd they say?" Fred asked from the back seat.

"She gets off at ten," he answered, but was wondering why she hadn't mentioned this to him.

"So, she should be home," Fred said.

"Somebody's home," Black pointed out as he pulled up in front of Brenda's house, after egressing the street from the opposite direction. There was a green four-door old model car sitting in front of James' house.

Black cut the engine. They all sat quietly, watching the house. James didn't need a scientist to explain this scenario to him. He'd already suspected Kim of messing around. This just validated it, but like the axiom goes: *If you go looking for something, eventually you'll find it.*

He was furious, not because she was messing around hell, he did the same, but because this bitch had been having unprotected sex with God knows who, got pregnant, and was endeavoring to put the baby off on him. James didn't really have a plan, although, at this moment, he wanted to just burst in on them with guns blazing, he knew he had to play it smart. He'd found out what he wanted to find out. Now he wanted to see who the baby's father really was.

'*I hate it for whoever the nigga is,*' Fred thought to himself as he fumbled the snub-nose .38 in his hands.

All James told him was that he wanted to catch Kim cheating. He didn't say what he was going to do once he'd found out. But Fred had known James long enough to know that they didn't always have to say what was on their minds. So, Fred didn't have to tell James that whatever he wanted to do to this nigga, he was all for it. Him being in the car was evident enough.

Black had not taken his eyes off the car since they'd pulled up. He recognized it as a Buick Lesabre. It didn't have any special effects to it, but he had a strong feeling he'd encountered the car at some point in time.

Moments later, a man emerged from the house, but being that it was dark out, they couldn't make out his features.

"Drive by so I can see this, nigga!" James told Black.

Black started the car, activated the lights, and approached the house at a slow pace. By that time, the man had reached his car, fumbling with his keys. When he looked up, they realized it was Mark, Ray's half-brother.

"This nigga gotta be suicidal!" James muttered as they rode by.

"Cause, he just committed suicide!"

## CHAPTER 22

The following day, Ray was awakened by his phone vibrating on the nightstand. That's when he noticed Tasha was no longer lying beside him. He did remember she had to go to work this morning, which was why he didn't plan on spending the night with her, but after she'd washed and re-braided his hair, he was too tired to go anywhere.

"Yeah?" he answered his phone.

"We need to talk," James sounded calm, but there was a hint of agitation in his voice.

"I'm listening."

"Not on the phone, Ray."

"Where you wanna meet at?"

"I'm in Knight Park," he told Ray. "I'll be out here all day."

"A'ight, I'll swing through later."

Ending the call, Ray placed the phone back on the stand and looked at the spot Tasha had occupied. There, on the pillow, was a piece of paper with a single key in the center of it. He picked the piece of paper up letting the key slide off onto the pillow. The piece of paper was a letter that read:

*Hello, Sleepy-head,*

*You don't know how bad I wanted to call in sick. So, I could get another dose of that good dick, but I have patients to tend to, and bills to pay. I'm sure you understand. N-E-Way, here's a spare key to my apartment, so you can 'cum' as you please. Look at it as the key to my heart. It's all yours! ~Love, Tasha~*

Yeah, right!" he said, laughing to himself.

After showering, he left Tasha's apartment, heading for his own, so he could change clothes and make for Knight Park. It was Saturday, and the weather was exceptional. So, there was going to be something of a Bland Town/Knight Park reunion, but Ray was anxious to hear what James wanted to talk to him about.

It was after eleven o'clock when Ray pulled into Maple Creek Parking. He approached his apartment door, where an envelope was stuck in the burglar bar door. He grabbed it but didn't read the letter it contained until he was inside his apartment. The letter read:

*I heard about your new 'girl-toy.' How old is she—fourteen? I guess I'll be bringing your daughter to visit you in prison, huh? When she gets older, I'll have to explain to her that her father is locked up for child molestation, because he couldn't tell the difference between a child and a grown woman!*

Ray was in a somewhat good mood, and he decided that he would not let this bitch change that. He already knew Connie was going to run her mouth about Half Pint— so, what! He balled the letter up, tossed it in the kitchen's trash, then headed for his bedroom to get dressed. *Fuck Sylvia and Connie!*

After changing clothes and putting something on his stomach, he was out the door, en-route to Knight Park. Arriving, he was surprised to see the number of people he was seeing at the recreational center which was called Knight Park, being that the neighborhood was originally known as Howell Station.

Ray parked behind a gold Cadillac Deville, belonging to Mr. Gold Digger. As he got out and ambled towards the ball court, where a game was underway, and people were gathered around, watching and placing bets. He looked around for Fred's car but didn't see it.

Now, he was thinking he should have driven around to Fred's place, first, but since he was here, he figured he might as well mingle with some of his old peers. Especially Mr. Gold Digger, who'd always have a slew of hoe stories to tell him.

\*\*\*

"Nigga, them ain't no dubs!" James objected when the dealer pulled a handful of small bags of marijuana from a Ziploc bag. He, Black and Fred had journeyed to the Bluff, in search of some weed even though Fred didn't smoke.

"You can buy or don't buy!" the dealer voiced, dumping the small bags back into the Ziploc.

180

"Make us some kind of deal," Black, who was standing beside James, said to the dealer.

"Ain't no deals!" he said. "I got a family to feed!"

"I'll give you fifty for three bags," James said, now fed up with this dude, and still pissed about last night.

"Apparently you don't hear too well!" the man spat. "What part of—"

Before he could finish his question, the palm of James' hand struck the side of the guy's face with a force that compelled him backward. He had a gun, but before he could reach for it, James had the Glock aimed at his chest.

"Since your stupid ass won't comply," James started, "I'ma take *all* that shit! Now lay your bitch ass on the ground!"

Fred who was across the street leaning against the black Oldsmobile had been watching the whole scene. He wasn't a bit surprised at what was transpiring. Hell, he was just happy to have his comrade back on the streets.

***

"So, what'd you do 'bout that, pimpin'?" Ray asked Mr. Gold Digger.

They were standing beyond the fence that outlined the basketball court. Two of Mr. Gold Digger's hoes were standing with them.

"What I do 'bout it?" asked Mr. Gold Digger, who was clad in a dark blue suit and matching alligator-skin loafers. "I put that bitch out on eighty-five and made that bitch walk back to the palace!"

"Where is she now?" Ray asked, now realizing one of the girls were missing.

"The bitch is on punishment," the procurer answered. "Enough about that two-dollar hoe. When are you fuckin' with my campaign again?"

Ray looked over at the two girls who were making sexual gestures towards him as if the question was their cue. The one that stuck her tongue out, touching the tip of her nose, had his full attention.

"How can a man resist a tongue like that?"

The voice had come from behind Ray. He turned to see James approaching, smoking a blunt.

"I don't mean to interrupt," James said. "But I need to borrow my brotha for a minute."

"So, what the move is?" Ray asked as he and James walked past the line of cars, nearing the rental Fred and Black were leaning against.

"I got some business I need to take care of," James told him. "But I wanna run it by you first."

"To see if I agree with it?"

"Not really."

Ray greeted Fred and Black, once they'd approached the car, and quickly obtained the notion that something was amiss. He looked over at James, who was taking a long drag on his blunt.

Seeing the look on Ray's face, he exhaled a portion of the smoke and said, "I found out some disturbing shit last night."

Saying nothing, Ray sat up on the hood of the car and waited for his brother to resume. Instead, James took another long pull on his blunt, finishing it. After thumping the stub and holding in the smoke for what seemed like an eternity, he exhaled, then gave Ray the rundown on last night's event.

"You spared that nigga," James continued, "I can't do it!"

It was only a few minutes after four, and Ray couldn't believe he was on his way home well, at least headed in that direction. What he really couldn't believe, was that Kim would even stoop that low, knowing how much he and James detested that nigga. How could she sleep with the enemy? The moment that question entered his mind, another one ensued: How long has she been sleeping with the enemy?

\*\*\*

"Park right here," James told Fred.

It was almost ten, James figured it would be best to stake out before ten, just in case Kim decided to leave early, complaining of pain or sickness, due to her pregnancy. Fred parked in front of Brenda's next-door neighbor's house, being that there was a car parked in front of hers. As he killed the engine, James dialed a number on his cellular.

"Burger King!" the familiar voice answered. "Donna speaking."

James asked, "May I speak to, Kim?"

"She already left," Donna said.

Just then, the Buick's headlights flashed through the windshield of the Oldsmobile as it entered the neighborhood, heading in their direction. James ended the call and snapped his cell phone shut, then they stooped low in the car to avoid being seen. They maintained their positions until Mark initiated a U-turn and drove by again.

Re-positioning themselves, they watched as Kim and Mark exited the car and headed for the house. James felt his anger grow as he observed the scene, looking from the bulge under Kim's uniformed shirt, to the nigga who would've been a dead-man-walking, had Ray not talked him out of it. He still couldn't apprehend why Ray had spared this nigga's life. Well, it really didn't matter because, after tonight, he was going to *wish* he was dead!

***

"Fred—Jay!"

Black, who was sitting in the back seat, delivered light blows to the two front seats they'd reclined and fallen asleep in. Coming to, they both sat up and saw what Black was seeing, Mark, leaving the house.

"Shit, he might as well had spent the night," James said after checking his watch, seeing that it was almost one o'clock.

They watched as he got into his car and approached MLK Drive. Fred waited until Mark made a left, before starting the rental, being that the headlights were automated, and he didn't want to chance Mark catching a glimpse of them.

Getting on the main road, Fred waited until Mark's car had disappeared around the curve, before initiating the tail at a respectable distance. They already knew he was going to take MLK to H.E. Holmes, and H.E. Holmes to Bankhead Highway, but the damage wouldn't be done until they reached Bowen Homes.

As they neared Bowen Homes, Fred closed the gap, so he was directly behind Mark. When they reached the security check, where they let him drive on, being that he was a resident.

"License!" one of the guards demanded.

Fred handed his fake license to the guard, who did a once over and handed it back. Before either of the guards could ask them who they were visiting at one in the morning, Fred rolled the window up and drove on, turning on Wilkes Circle.

"Just park on the street," James told him.

As soon as Fred parked, they quickly dismounted, conveying wooden baseball bats as they moved briskly towards Walden Street, hoping to catch Mark before he made it inside the apartment. Crossing the vast yard, they surveyed the area for late-night wanderers. It was all clear.

When they made it to the gateless fence that sundered Wilkes Circle and Walden Street, they saw that Mark had already pulled into the parking lot but was still sitting in the car with the engine running, talking on the phone.

As James took the lead, they filed through the gate and approached the end apartment door, which was two doors down from Mark's like they were visiting that residence. It was obvious Mark had seen them, but their movements shouldn't have alarmed him, considering they held their bats to their sides, out of his view.

Once they were behind the concrete wall that contained a clothesline for the end and adjacent apartments, they pulled out ski masks. Fred, who had systematized the plot, pulled out a small can of O.C. spray. Hearing the car's engine shut off, Fred and James peered through one of the many huge, carved-out slits in the wall. Mark exited the car, coming their way.

"Let's do it," Fred said as they donned their masks.

Once Mark was as close as they wanted him, Fred, followed by James and Black, darted from the opposite side of the wall in which they'd entered.

"What the f—" was all Mark could manage, before Fred blinded him with the spray, and quickly stepped aside.

Mark cried out, bringing his hands to his face, taking steps back. Wasting no time, James holding the bat as if he was waiting for the pitch, swung with all his might, fracturing Mark's knuckles, right along with his nose.

Playa Ray

## CHAPTER 23

"Why can't y'all get jobs like ordinary people?"

Ray and James exchanged glances, then looked across the table at their mother who'd posed the question.

"James, you have to think about that baby," she continued. "Don't let him—"

"Can we talk about this some other time, mama?" James interrupted, looking around at Robert and his son, Raymond who'd joined them for Sunday dinner. James hadn't said two words to either of them.

"When did April say she was coming down?" Ray asked, hoping to prevent a quarrel between his mother and brother, being that he was duly aware of James' bad mood the moment he'd picked him up in Knight Park. He wanted to ask James about last night but thought against it. He was tempted to turn on the T.V. this morning, to see if it had made the news, but dismissed the thought, knowing he would find out eventually.

"In three weeks," Mary answered, casting a glance at Raymond causing Ray to do likewise. Perhaps she too had noticed how acquainted he and April had gotten on her last visit.

Hearing the phone ring, Mary excused herself and headed for her bedroom to answer it.

"So, what kind of skills would I need to tow cars, Mr. Robert?" Ray asked.

"None," Robert answered. "All you need is your driver's license. I could show you how to operate the gears on the truck, which is easy.

"And how easy would it be for me to get the job?"

"The manager and I are best friends," Robert smiled and winked his eye at Ray.

Just then, Mary re-entered the kitchen with her hand over her chest, and tears welling up in her eyes.

"What's wrong, sweetheart?" Robert asked her.

"Your brotha's in the hospital," she spoke, looking directly at Ray, then went to explain that Mark's mother told her that Mark was beaten profusely in front of their apartment, by a group of unidentified men with bats, that left the bones in his legs, hands, and nose broken. His skull was also fractured, which doctors deemed a metal plate would have to be installed. "Ray, go and see him."

"For what?" Ray asked, not at all astounded that she would advise him to do something she knew he was not going to do.

He looked at James, who was tending to his food as if he hadn't heard a word of the conversation.

Mary persisted. "I'll go with you."

"I'm not going, mama!" Ray was now furious.

Detecting Ray's anger, Mary took a seat and allowed the tears to roll down her cheeks. Robert moved in to console her.

"I'm out," Ray announced, getting up from the table and entering the living room.

He put on his windbreaker and exited the house. It took several attempts to start his car, but the moment the engine came alive, James slid into the passenger seat.

"You aight, lil' bruh?" James asked.

"I'm cool," Ray lied, not looking in his brother's direction.

"You know how she is," said James. "She looks at them like they're family. So, you can pretty much imagine how she feels about that shit."

"Yeah." Ray was insensitive at this moment.

"Now, I gotta deal with Kim's disrespectful ass," James spoke, holding his hand to a vent in search of heat. When he noticed the look Ray was giving him, he said, "Don't worry, I'm not gonna kill the bitch."

\*\*\*

"Here this bitch is now," James announced to Fred and Black.

He was peering through the Venetian blind in the living room window when Patrice's car pulled up in front of the house. He didn't know how he did it, but as angry as he was about the whole ordeal. He found himself smiling when Kim and Patrice bolted from the car and stood baffled at the sight of Kim's belongings strewed all over the lawn.

"She's about to call the police," Black, who was now looking through the blinds, said as Kim pulled out her cellular.

It didn't take long for James to grasp that. Black parked his car up the street, so, from the girls' point of view, it pretty much looked like the house had been burglarized. So, not wasting another second, James followed by his comrades, made for the front door. They stepped outside and stood on the porch. Although it was dark out, James was still able to see the apprehension on Kim's face.

"James!" Kim exclaimed but kept her distance. "What happened?"

"Get your shit out my yard!" he said struggling to keep his composure, though he really wanted to choke this bitch out.

"What's wrong, James?" she pleaded.

"Get your shit out my yard!" he reiterated. "And don't bring your trifling ass back over here."

***

After leaving his mother's house, Ray drove straight home although he was tempted to drive through Hollywood Courts to see if he could spot Half Pint, who hadn't returned any of his calls.

Now, he was soaking in the bathtub, where he'd been for almost an hour, and for some odd reason, he could not stop thinking about Sylvia. His feelings for her had never subsided, but his main concern was the baby. There was no doubt in his mind that the child was his.

The sound of someone knocking on his door brought him out of his reverie.

"Damn!" he said to himself, wishing for the umpteenth time he'd never started trapping out of his apartment.

He didn't plan on inviting anyone in or opening the door for that matter, so he just wrapped a towel around him, and headed for the front door, where he peered through the glass to see Kim staring back at him. Saying nothing, he opened the door, then headed for his bedroom, where he put on one of his robes. He re-entered the living room and saw that Kim had taken a seat on the sofa. Her coat was unbuttoned, revealing she was still in uniform. He could also tell that she'd been crying.

"What's up?" he asked, standing with his arms folded.

"James put me out," she said with little emotion. "When I got home, he had—"

"Why?" he cut in.

"I don't know."

"So, you're not gonna tell me the truth?"

Her expression showed that the question caught her off guard.

"How long has that shit been going on?" Ray continued.

She just stared at him. The tears that were welling up in her eyes, began cascading down her face. "For a while," she finally admitted.

"What the fuck is *a while*, Kim!" The love and respect he had for Kim, was no more. Now he wanted this bitch out of his apartment, and out of his life as well.

"Almost a year," she answered wiping tears from her eyes.

That did it! Ray could not stand to look at this bitch another second, but he couldn't kick her out without asking. "So, whose baby is it?"

Just the thought of answering the question must've hurt, because she dropped her head and confessed, "I don't know."

"Bye Kim," Ray turned, heading for his bedroom. "You can let yourself out."

He entered his room, then stopped and listened as the front door opened and closed.

## CHAPTER 24

It had only been a week since James' release, and they'd already come up on a trap house to hit. Now, James, Black, Fred, and Ray were sitting in a stolen car, parked a few houses away from the one they'd been watching for four days. They'd already known about the house, and the traffic had been the same since they'd been watching it.

"There they go!" James, who was seated in the front passenger seat said when he'd spotted the Ford Explorer approaching the house and pull into the driveway. Three men dismounted, retrieved three duffle bags, from the cargo area and approached the front door, vigilantly. "Relocate!" James told Black, once the men entered the house.

Black stuck the flat-head screwdriver into the left side of the steering column to start it. Not using the headlights, he parked the car directly across the street from the house and killed the engine.

Ray, who was seated behind Black was looking at the house, but his mind was on the message Tasha left on his voicemail earlier. He could still hear the urgency in her voice as the message played back in his head. *"Ray, we need to talk, face to face!"*

"Ray?" James pulled his brother from his abstract musing, seeing that he looked a bit disturbed.

"What's up?" Ray answered.

"You a'ight?"

"Yeah, I'm cool."

"Here she comes y'all!" Fred spotted the Infiniti as it made its way towards them. They stooped as low as they could until the car pulled into the driveway, parking behind the Ford. "Stick to the script, and no unnecessary bloodshed!" he told them.

They watched as the woman dismounted and began unstrapping her baby from the car seat in the back seat. That was their cue. They all donned ski masks and exited the car, conveying the guns Fred purchased before James' arrest. The woman had managed to free her baby from the car seat, but by the time she stood erect with the baby in her arms, there were two pistol-grip pumps and two AK-47 assault rifles aimed just inches away at different parts of her body.

"That's a quick way to get killed!" James told the woman who looked like she was about to call all cars. "All you gotta do is cooperate," he said.

Initiating his part of the plan, Black lowered the AK and reached for the baby.

"No— please!" she pleaded, turning her back on them to parry whatever harm was to happen her child.

James was not hearing this shit. The plan was to get in and out as quick as possible, but right now, this bitch was making it difficult to do so. So, not in the mood to negotiate any further, James yanked the infant from the woman's grasp and shoved it at Black, who managed to catch him before he hit the ground.

"Shut the fuck up!" James told the woman, who was pleading for her baby's life again. "Let's go!"

"Go where?" she asked with fear in her eyes.

"This way," James grabbed her by her coat's collar and ushered her towards the house. "Where your keys?"

She held out a key ring with no more than five keys. "Right here."

"Where them niggas at?"

"They're always in the back room."

"Always?"

"Yes."

"So, they would be there, right now?"

"Yes."

"Open the door!" James demanded, still holding onto her coat.

As if the child could feel what was about to take place. He started crying the moment his mother stuck the key into the lock.

"Can I have, my baby?" she begged.

"As soon as you open this door."

Wasting no more time, she did as she was required. As soon as the door swung open, James shoved her through the threshold, with the intent to use her as a shield, just in case these dudes were on point. As they rushed in with their weapons at the ready, they saw that the living room was empty. Fred quickly surveyed the kitchen it was also, empty.

"Sit down and shut that baby up!" James ordered the woman.

Despite the situation she was currently facing, she was more than happy to receive her baby from the masked man who clearly needed lessons on how to hold a baby. Once she'd taken a seat on the sofa to console her child, Ray placed his back against the front door to keep an eye on her. While James, Fred, and Black journeyed to the back room for the three men.

As Fred led, they did a quick survey of the first two rooms standing wide open. They were empty. The last room was just beyond the small bathroom. The door was closed, but as they stood in front of it, they could hear indistinct chatter amongst the guys on the other side. Fred looked to his comrades. Once they'd nodded indicating they were ready. Fred turned the knob and thrust the door open.

"Get up!" Fred demanded the three men sitting in foldable chairs at a foldable table which were the only means of furniture in the room, that contained scales, cutting boards, kilos of cocaine, and a large black trash bag containing marijuana, the smell permeated the small room.

The men raised their hands up and slowly stood to their feet. Fred and Black kept their guns aimed, while James conducted a pat down, recovering two handguns off two of them, placing them on the table. James then nodded at Black, who backed out of the room, with his gun still leveled on the men.

"Follow him!" James ordered, nudging one of the guys in the side with the barrel of the pistol-grip pump.

As the men filed out of the room, Fred and James trailed behind. Once they got to the living room, the men were ordered to lie face down on the floor.

"What about her?" Black nodded towards the female, who was still holding the baby who appeared to be asleep.

"You plan on babysitting?"

Ray's question caught Black by surprise because he just stared at Ray. Already knowing where this was going, James stepped over the men and grabbed the woman's pocketbook that was sitting beside her on the sofa. Perusing the bag, he pulled out a black .25 automatic and tossed it to Ray, who surveyed it, then dropped it into his back pocket.

"Let's get this shit over with!" James said, dropping the pocketbook on the table, then heading for the main bedroom to conduct his search, while Fred took the child's room.

Black handed Ray the AK he was carrying and proceeded to bind the men with a roll of duct tape. Ray looked over at the woman, who to his surprise was watching him. She was notably attractive, but that was beyond Ray. He was thinking had James not found that gun in her pocketbook.

"Lay the baby on the sofa!" Ray told her. Once she'd obeyed, he had her join the men on the floor, where her arms and legs were also bonded.

\*\*\*

An hour later, the crew was back at James' house, seated at the kitchen table, sorting out everything. There were ten kilos of cocaine, the trash bag full of marijuana, and three shoe boxes. One containing stacks of twenty-dollar bills, another containing fifty-dollar bills and stacks of one-hundred-dollar bills in the last one of over fifty-six thousand dollars.

"Them niggas ran a nice lil' operation!" Fred commented.

"Yeah, they were getting it in," Ray agreed.

James asked, "Fred you're on the pots, right?"

"You know it!"

"What about the money?" Black wanted to know.

Fred looked around at his allies before speaking. "Everybody gets five stacks. We'll find a spot to stash the rest. Whatever we make off the product, goes into the stash. Ray, you handle the weed, ounces, and pounds. It's our time to step it up. We just gotta do it together."

"We're gonna do more than step it up," James said, leaning forward with his elbows on the table. "We're taking over!"

## CHAPTER 25

It had been two weeks, and the crew was starting to see progress. Ray had damn near the whole Westside flocking to his apartment for pounds and ounces of weed. He'd even referred some dealers to his crew to cop ounces of cocaine. James would drop off an ounce of cocaine to Steve, on Campbellton Road, to keep his trap going. Black had gone back to Capital Homes and put two of his ex-trap buddies on.

He decided to uphold his dime trap in Chapel Forest and to let Fred and James deal the weight. Fred tried to get Poncho and the other dealers in Edgewood to shop with them, but they declined, claiming they'd stick with their current suppliers. Drop Squad, of course.

"Y'all go ahead and grab a table," James told his homies, once they entered Club Body Tap. "I'll catch up."

It was Saturday, and they'd decided to treat themselves to a strip joint for some relaxation, after two weeks of hustling and strategizing.

"Evenin', my man!" James said to the D.J. upon entering the D.J.'s booth, handing him a fifty-dollar bill. "I need to make a public announcement if you don't mind."

"Not at all!" the D.J. answered, after surveying the bill and stuffing it into his pocket.

James looked out at everybody below. After spotting his crew taking a seat at a table by the stage. He nodded at the D.J., who killed the music before leaning the mike towards him.

"Evenin', ladies and gents!" he spoke into the mike. "For those of you who don't know who I am—I'm King James, bitch! And the Kingz are in the building! Thank you very much!"

Satisfied with his announcement, James exited the booth and set out to join the rest.

"King James, huh?" Fred said when James rejoined them.

"Hell yeah!" James replied. "And why are we not in VIP?"

"It's already occupied."

"Shit, we can buy them, niggas, out!"

"I doubt that."

"What'd you mean you—" James looked up at the VIP booth, where five men were being entertained by five dancers. He didn't have to make out the emblems on the chains to know who they were.

Black was also looking up at the booth, but it was not the men who held his attention. It was the blonde, red-bone who was slow grinding on one of the men laps. He'd already accepted the fact, that she worked here, but to actually see her half-naked, dancing in another man's lap, did something to him.

"Can we dance for the Kingz?" The crew looked back to see two dancers smiling down on them.

"What was that?" James asked, pretending he hadn't heard correctly.

"Can we dance for the Kingz?" one of the girls reiterated.

"Yeah, y'all can dance for the Kingz," James told them. "But first, y'all gotta tell me who I am."

"King James, bitch!" they said in unison.

James smiled at his comrades. They didn't know that a part of his plans was beginning to unfold.

*** 

"Daddy, my teacher has a parakeet."

Black was staring across the Burger King's dining area at Nikki and Willie who looked old enough to be Nikki's father as they playfully fed each other across the table. It was Sunday afternoon, and Nikki and the kids would be headed back to Florida within an hour. Black had enjoyed the weekend with his kids, but there were things he wanted to say to Nikki. Things he couldn't and wouldn't dare say in the presence of her new man.

"You heard me, Daddy?"

Black looked across the table at his adorable daughter, who was staring back at him with her mother's eyes. "I heard you, baby."

"What did I say?" she asked, folding her arms over her chest.

"You said something about a parrot."

"Parakeet!" she corrected.

"And what's the difference between a parrot and a parakeet?" he challenged, feeding applesauce to Lil' Keith, who was strapped into a high chair.

"A parakeet is a small parrot."

"And what's a parrot?" Black smiled, anticipating her answer.

"A parrot is a big parakeet," she smiled back at him.

For some reason, Black knew she was going to say that. He laughed so hard, it brought tears to his eyes. He couldn't believe how much he'd missed his babies. All three of them.

After saying his goodbyes, he left Burger King and headed home to spend some time with, Connie.

"Hey, baby!" Connie greeted him when he entered the front door. "How are the kids?"

"They cool," he answered. Then seeing Meeka, Sylvia and Star sitting in the living room, he said, "What up, y'all!"

Black had not spoken directly to Sylvia since the break-up between her and Ray. Connie asked him not to tell Ray that Sylvia had been visiting on the weekends. He didn't, but if Ray so happened to ask, Black would be more than happy to tell him about that slut and her *girlfriend* Star.

He didn't make eye contact with either of them as he headed for the bedroom, removing his coat.

"You okay?" Connie entered the room behind him, took his coat, and hung it in the closet.

"I'm good, baby girl." He kissed her on the lips, then sat on the bed to take his shoes off. "I'ma lay down for a minute."

"You still gotta meet up with your boys later?"

"Yeah.'

\*\*\*

As he pulled up to Eric's house, Fred parked on the street, behind Curt's silver Acura. Before he could knock on the front door, it swung open.

Welcome to hell!" Sharonda dramatized, revealing large plastic vampire teeth in her mouth.

Fred looked at his watch. "You got one more week, Sharonda."

"I'm just practicing," she said, after taking the plastic teeth out. "Did I scare you?"

"Yeah, I think I peed on myself."

She laughed. "Shut up fool and come on in!"

"They in the kitchen?" he asked as he entered.

"Yeah."

Eric and Curt were seated at the kitchen table. Eric was weighing cocaine on his scale.

"What's up, lil homie!" Curt regarded Fred.

"I can't call it," Fred answered, giving him dap, then taking a seat.

"That's three and a baby," Eric asserted as he pulled the last piece off the scale and handed it to Curt, who placed it inside a Ziploc bag. "They're waiting on you now."

"A'ight." Curt gathered the product and made his exit.

"How's business?" Eric asked his brother, once Curt left.

"Slow, but better," he answered. "We got a few customers."

"It's four of y'all," Eric told him. "If y'all stay down, y'all can turn that shit into an empire, but it won't happen overnight."

"Yeah, I know. What's the deal on the barbershop?"

"I sign the papers tomorrow."

"You're gonna rename it?"

Nah, I like Hair Masters."

\*\*\*

"I believe you would make a good lawyer," Raymond said to April, who was seated beside him at the kitchen table.

April smiled at the compliment. "You think so?"

"Man, I know you're not falling for that weak-ass game!" James, who was seated beside Ray, asserted. He'd been listening to Raymond's adoring remarks ever since they all sat down to eat.

Everyone looked in James' direction, including Ray, who hadn't been paying attention to either of them, because he was too busy mulling over what Tasha told him about moving back to

Chicago and wanting him to come with her. Since then, he'd been feeling like *Kane* from the movie *Menace to Society,* when Ronnie had asked him to move to Atlanta with her.

"I'm just playing lil sis," James lied. "At least he got a decent job."

James delved into his meatloaf, disregarding the looks they were giving him, but at the same time, his mind was at work. Maybe Raymond could come in handy someday.

"When is my nephew due?" April asked.

"And why haven't you brought Kim over lately?" Mary wanted to know.

"I don't know," James answered, not looking up from his plate.

"To which question?" asked Mary.

"Both," he answered, now looking around the table. "Any other questions?"

Seeing that there were no more questions, James looked at his watch and reminded Ray of the meeting with Fred and Black. They said their goodnights and headed for James' house. After Fred and Black arrived, they all assembled at the kitchen table, where there were wooden jewelry boxes sitting in front of each of them.

"Y'all can go ahead and open 'em," James told his comrades as he opened the one in front of him.

They all pulled out white gold chains with large emblems that read: *'Kingz!'*

"Yeah, I used money from the stash," James admitted, conceding Fred's inquisitive look. "We'll get it back. Besides, it went to a good cause. It's part of the movement."

"Movement?" asked Fred.

"I can't explain until y'all accept those," James said, slipping the chain over his head. Once they'd followed suit, James stood and avowed. "We're about to step this shit up, and I feel that we should have a name to go with the fame."

"The Kingz, huh?" said Black.

"Yes, King Black," James affirmed. "As Kingz, we are all equal."

Fred nodded.

"King Ray?" James regarded his brother.
"I'm in."
"King Black?"
"Shit let's get it!"
They all stood and shook hands to solidify the new movement.

# CHAPTER 26

It was the second week of December, and the Kingz had been on a rampage. They'd robbed two more drug houses, and planted workers in Carver Homes, Herdon Homes, Perry Homes, Mechanicsville, Summer Hill, Thomasville Heights, and on Cleveland Avenue.

They had also leased BMW's of the same make and model, replacing the cars emblems with golden crowns. Each car was equipped with chrome twenty-two-inch rims, sound systems, and three T.V. screens, so they would all be equal, except for the brand of rims and color of the exterior and interior. James' colors were purple and black, Ray's colors were black on black, Fred's colors were dark-green and tan and Black's colors were dark-blue and black.

"Man, where this nigga at?" Fred asked checking his watch.

The Kingz were all in Fred's bedroom, waiting on B.J. to deliver the hot box they were going to use in tonight's robbery in Riverdale.

"See what's up, Ray," said James, checking his own watch.

Ray pulled out his cell phone to dial B.J.'s number when it started vibrating.

"Where you at?" Ray answered it.

"I just turned on Niles," B.J. informed.

"A'ight." Ray hung up and turned to his crew. "It's on us."

At that, the Kingz, who were already clad in dark clothing, gathered their artillery and trotted through the kitchen to the back door. Since Fred's mother was sitting in the living room, watching T.V. They made it to Herdon Street, just as a black four door Cadillac, followed by B.J.'s Chevy, came into view. B.J., who was driving the Cadillac, stopped in front of them and got out.

"It hasn't been reported yet," B.J. told them.

"It wouldn't matter," Fred replied, paying B.J. the five hundred dollars as negotiated.

Once the exchange was made, the Kingz were on their way to Riverdale, Georgia. It was well after one a.m. when Ray parked the

Cadillac across the street from the targeted house. Now they would have to wait on the drop, which was every Wednesday, after midnight.

The headlights of the minivan shone through the back window of the Cadillac, but they didn't try to avoid the rays. Instead, they donned their masks and bolted from the car, carrying handguns as the van entered the driveway, parking behind a white Mercedes Benz. James and Ray approached the driver's side as Fred and Black took the opposite.

Almost simultaneously, James and Fred snatched the front doors open. Ray and Black slid open the two rear doors.

"Step on out!" James told the two White male occupants.

As the men sagely dismounted, Black carried three gym bags to the Cadillac. Ray watched the house for any signs of movement, while Fred and James searched the men, who were unarmed. Once Black returned, they ushered the men up to the front door.

"We already know y'all got a special knock," Fred told them. "Do anything other than that knock, y'all can cancel Christmas!"

The driver took that into consideration and initiated the knock. Fred looked to Ray for ratification, Ray nodded. The Kingz stepped aside as the man beyond the door peered through the peephole to confirm his guests. When the lock clicked, and the door opened partially, Fred and James forced the men inside and onto the floor. There were two black men present, the one who'd opened the door, and another sitting on the sofa, running bills through a counter.

"Y'all know what it is!" James announced. "Hit the floor!"

While the men were cooperating, Black and Ray set off to check the other rooms for occupants. All the rooms were empty. They made it back to the living room, where James was stuffing the piles of bills that were on the table, inside a gym bag. Completing that task, he zipped it shut and tossed it to Ray, who dropped it by the front door. Then, James and Fred set off to search the rest of the house, while Black proceeded to duct tape the men.

In one bedroom, Fred flipped mattresses, pulled out dresser drawers and everything from the closet. All he found were two handguns, four ounces of weed, some jewelry, and a wad of bills, in which he stuffed into the tote bag he'd brought with him. As he left the room, he peered into the room James entered. James appeared to be taking his time, so Fred made for the next room.

James had already rummaged through the closet, finding a shoebox full of bills, and a .44 Desert Eagle in which he stuffed into his tote bag. When he flipped the mattress, he saw a pistol-grip pump he had no intentions of taking. Disregarding the jewelry atop the dresser, he commenced to rummaging through the drawers, one at a time, until something in one drawer caught his attention, stopping him in his tracks.

Once Black had duct taped the last man, Ray handed him back his gun and glanced at his watch. They'd been in the house longer than expected.

The second he thought it, James emerged from the room, briskly. Ray sensed something was wrong, but it was confirmed when James aimed the .44 Desert Eagle he'd found and fired a slug into the back of all four of the men's heads. This move stunned Ray and Black. Fred rushed from the back on high alert. For a moment, they all just stared down at the cadavers.

Let's ride!" James broke the ice, tossing the gun on the sofa.

The drive back to Atlanta seemed to take forever as they rode in silence. Once returning to Bland Town, Ray pulled behind an abandoned warehouse, where they were going to ditch the Cadillac and hike the railroad tracks back to Knight Park. Once Ray parked, they all dismounted and just stood around.

Fred looked over at James, who had his back to them. He wanted to question the stunt James pulled back at the house but held his peace. He knew he could beat James at any form of fighting, but right now, James was furious and strapped!

"Why'd you off them folks, Jay?" Ray asked, looking over the car at his brother.

"I had to," James stated placidly, back still turned.

"They were tied up," Fred avowed. "They didn't pose a threat."

"Y'all don't understand," James told them.

"Well, help us to understand!" Ray was becoming agitated. James was beginning to remind him of Bishop from the movie *Juice*.

James was slowly shaking his head. "I don't know. It might be best if y'all let it go."

"You're not making sense, Jay," Fred told him. "That's un-kinglike."

Hearing this, James gave in. Approaching the rear of the car, he extracted a shiny item from his tote bag and carefully placed it on the trunk. The other Kingz gathered around to gander at the chain with the ominous pendant.

# CHAPTER 27

For two weeks, the Kingz had been keeping a low profile, but the product was still circulating through the guys they had working under them. There were twenty kilos of cocaine, and over seven hundred and twenty thousand taken from the last robbery. Each King received a hundred thousand and stashed the rest of the money and drugs at James' house, which was known as The *Palace*.

Two weeks of laying low were enough time for the Kingz to strategize their next moves and do some Christmas shopping, but neither of them was too fond of all work and no play. Therefore, they decided to attend the Christmas Eve party at Club Stokers. They weren't worried about Drop Squad, because there was no way to prove they had anything to do with the demise of one of their affiliates, but they did have four, heavily-armed Kingzmen tailing their stretched Ford Excursion tonight, just in case.

As the limousine inched along, they scanned the crowded parking lot, looking for Curt, who was to meet them in front of the club to pick up a package. They'd hired Curt to transport for them when he was not transporting for Eric, who was now buying his weight from the Kingz.

"I don't see him," Black asserted.

"He better be here!" Fred said, remembering how Eric used to complain about Curt's tardiness.

"There he is," Ray said once the truck stopped in front of the club.

Curt approached the truck from the left side, flashing his signal of acknowledgment to the Kingzmen in the next truck as arranged, for security reasons.

"Same thing," Fred told Curt when he rolled down the window and handed him the shoulder bag.

When Curt departed, James tapped on the window for the driver who'd been patiently waiting on the right side to open the door for them. Being that celebrities are often spotted at Stokers, the people waiting in line to go inside were gawking at the Kingz as they exited the limousine. To see if they were a part of the who's who.

"That's a long ass line!" Black exclaimed.

"Too bad we won't be joining them," James said, starting towards the entrance, followed by the other Kingz, Kingzmen were to remain outside.

As they moved along the line, the people were admiring the Kingz emblems they'd had embellished with diamonds.

"Invitations—VIP Passes?" one of the bouncers asked.

"Yeah, we got all that," James handed both men five one-hundred-dollar bills. "Merry Christmas."

Realizing what they had, the bouncers exchanged glances and were more than happy to allow the Kingz entrance.

*Run DMC's 'A Christmas Carol'* was roaring through the club's speakers when they entered. Besides the strippers, party-goers were also dancing and having a good time. Some were even clad in Santa hats, coats, and even bushy white beards.

"Hold up! Wait one cotton-pickin' minute!" D.J. Spenz, who sold weed for the Kingz shouted over the music when he'd spotted them. "We got some more certified hood celebrities in this bitch! That's right, the Kingz are in the building! Y'all give it up for the Kingz!"

James was pleased by the introduction D.J. Spenz delivered, but he was quite astounded by the crowd's ovation. He could tell his crew was also, as they moved along, nodding and waving their appreciations.

James had intended to buy the VIP booth from the three men who were occupying it, but they declined and offered to share the booth with the Kingz.

"I'm Joe," the guy sitting beside Ray said offering his hand.

Joe was short, stocky, about 5'6" and weighed two-hundred and ten pounds, with salt and peppered hair that was pulled back into a ponytail. To Ray, Joe looked like he was getting the money.

"King Ray," Ray replied, shaking Joe's hand, then introducing the rest of the Kingz in that manner.

"The Kingz!" Joe asserted, nodding his head. "Y'all ringing in the South."

"That's where you from?" James asked, delighted to hear that they were getting recognition in Jonesboro South.

"Born and raised," Joe answered. "Now I'm in Douglasville."

"You hustle?" James wanted to know.

"I fuck with that white from time to time, but I mainly fuck with credit cards and checks."

"I brought the best in the house," the club owner stated and stepped aside to let seven dancers enter the booth. "Y'all play nice!" he added, then disappeared.

All men pulled out money as the dancers took their positions and conducted their sexual routines. While Fred was tipping the dancer, who was making her ass clap in his face. He kept a cautious eye on the crowd below. Ever since the last robbery, he'd been in a full state of paranoia, which was bad for business because he couldn't trust anyone he'd come in contact with. Drop Squad would go to the extreme to find any kind of information pertaining to the death of one of their own. Then, they would put an unimaginable price on the culprit's head.

"Awww shit!" D.J. Spenz yelled into the microphone. "Ladies get ready to drop it like it's hot! And speaking of *drop*, y'all gotta know Drop Squad is in this bitch!"

He didn't have to tell them to give it up for the infamous group they were already applauding. Had Fred known the bouncers were not going to search them, he would've brought his Glock in the club. Right now, he would wage anything that these niggas took full advantage of the special no-search treatment. They were strapped!

Fred didn't have to look to see if his crew were observing the eight members of the notorious mob because the whole club was watching. Now they were talking with the owner, who, after a few seconds, pointed up at the booth.

*** 

After making his drop in Clarkston, Curt made it back to Atlanta with the intent to get his rocks off, being that he didn't have to report back to the Kingz until tomorrow night. Despite the cold weather, prostitutes were still clinging to their posts on Metropolitan formerly known as Stewart Avenue especially his favorite girl, Honey. Who was always stationed in Mrs. Winner's parking lot. As always, her face lit up when Curt's Acura pulled in. She sprinted towards the car and climbed into the passenger seat.

"Hey baby!" she spoke, revealing four gold caps on her bottom teeth.

"You still chasing Christmas money?" he asked.

"Always, you, contributing?"

"You know I am."

"Well, to the bat cave!" she said, smiling.

Exiting the parking lot, Curt turned on Catheryn Street and drove up to the school he'd never known the name of, parking in front of it. Wasting no time, Honey undid his belt and pulled his pants and boxers to his ankles. He was already fully erect when she took him into her mouth.

Honey had the best head he'd ever encountered, but he would never tell her that. In fact, it was so good, he didn't see, or hear the black H-2 Hummer pull up behind them with the lights off. Two men dismounted from the rear-passenger seats, carrying AK-47s. They approached Curt's car one on each side, but he nor Honey had noticed because their eyes were closed.

Once the man on the passenger side nodded to the one on the driver side, they both squeezed their triggers, sending slugs through metal, glass, and flesh.

# CHAPTER 28

It was Christmas day, and the Kingz had decided to spend it with their families, then convene at the Palace at midnight.

Ray and James were to meet April, Mary, Robert and Raymond at their grandmother's house in Decatur.

Fred drove his mother out to Eric's place, where they were going to exchange gifts and enjoy the dinner Sharonda had prepared.

Black had sent gifts to his daughter in Virginia and held on to Lil' Keith's and Nicole's gifts, being that Nikki had planned to bring the kids to visit him tomorrow. This morning, he surprised Connie with three mink coats, designer boots, and a diamond ring he'd bought for her. Now he was on his way to Felicia's house to drop off Kevin's gifts.

Turning into the driveway, he parked behind Felicia's BMW and looked in the back seat at the pile of gift-wrapped presents he and Connie had spent all night wrapping, two nights ago.

'Kevin is definitely going to have to help carry these gifts inside,' he thought, dismounting. As he neared the front door, he noticed that it was slightly ajar. Perhaps they'd heard him pull up, and—

Black curbed that thought immediately. If they would've heard him pull up, Kevin would have bolted from the house like a bat out of hell, being that it was Christmas, and he knew that his daddy was not going to show up empty-handed. Plus, it was way too cold to even make the slightest mistake of leaving the door, or windows, slightly ajar.

Just in case that was the case, he lightly tapped on the door, then slowly pushed it open. What he saw caused his heart rate to expedite—the place was trashed!

Black reached his waist, then quickly remembered that he'd left his gun at home. He wanted to turn and leave, but something within him wouldn't permit it. All he could think about was his son. He had to see if his son was alright. After building enough courage, he cautiously entered the house, stepping over various debris, such as broken china, Christmas tree ornaments, the tree has also been abused, broken glass from the fish tank, and of course, the myriad fish that appeared to be still squirming—alive!

Black didn't know how long it took for a fish to die, once they'd been stripped of water, but he couldn't imagine them staying alive for more than ten minutes. He cautiously made his way down the hallway, approaching Felicia's bedroom, first. Just as he'd expected, her room had been ransacked. Feeling no need to enter, he made for Kevin's room, feeling nauseated, expecting the inevitable, but Kevin's room seemed to be untouched.

Black was extremely pissed off, but he managed to keep his composure, while he tried to sort things out. Felicia's car was in the driveway, the house had been ransacked, but neither one of them were here. It didn't take a scientist to conclude that they'd been kidnapped. But by who, had Drop Squad found out who'd killed their comrades?

Black doubted this because if that was so, they would have been waiting outside Stokers, last night, like a lynch mob. As he pondered that, he thought of how terrified he was when the Drop Squad members approached the VIP booth, last night. He had actually thought he was going to be murdered right there inside the club, in front of all those people, but that wasn't the case at all.

It just so happened that one of the dancers was the baby sister of one of the guys, and he didn't approve of what she was doing, so he demanded that she leave. They hashed it out for a brief moment before she gave in. Now Black fought back tears that had been welling up in his eyes as he re-entered the living room. As he stopped and re-assessed the damage, he pulled out his cellular and called Fred, only to get his voicemail. He then called James.

"This better be important!" James came in on the other end.

"It is," Black said, hearing his own voice crack. "Somebody kidnapped Felicia and Kevin."

"What!" James exclaimed, in disbelief. "Where you at?"

"I'm at her crib, right now," Black answered. "Somebody had—"

The sound of glass being stepped on behind him, caused him to stop mid-sentence, but before he could turn to see who or what had caused the noise, he was struck in the head by some kind of metal object, which instantly rendered him unconscious.

To Be Continued...
*Kingz of the Game 2*
Coming Soon

## About the Author

*Playa Ray was born Norris Ray McCoy on November 23, 1979, and raised in Atlanta, Georgia. Growing up in the poverty-stricken abode, promoted a young Ray into inadvertently discovering talents he'd never dreamed of possessing, whereas music had become his first love. He was always one with a vivid imagination, so the aspiring musician tried his hand at writing screenplays, in hopes of creating stories that people could actually watch on their very own televisions. Now currently incarcerated, the author spends his time writing books of all genres, with the same hopes of welcoming you into the mind of a paragon. You can follow the author on Facebook and Instagram at Norris McCoy!*

# Submission Guideline

Submit the first three chapters of your completed manuscript to ldpsubmissions@gmail.com, subject line: Your book's title. The manuscript must be in a .doc file and sent as an attachment. Document should be in Times New Roman, double spaced and in size 12 font. Also, provide your synopsis and full contact information. If sending multiple submissions, they must each be in a separate email.

Have a story but no way to send it electronically? You can still submit to LDP/Ca$h Presents. Send in the first three chapters, written or typed, of your completed manuscript to:

**LDP: Submissions Dept**
**Po Box 870494**
**Mesquite, Tx 75187**

*DO NOT send original manuscript. Must be a duplicate.*

Provide your synopsis and a cover letter containing your full contact information.

Thanks for considering LDP and Ca$h Presents.

**Coming Soon from Lock Down Publications/Ca$h Presents**

BOW DOWN TO MY GANGSTA

By **Ca$h**

TORN BETWEEN TWO

By **Coffee**

BLOOD STAINS OF A SHOTTA **III**

By **Jamaica**

STEADY MOBBIN **III**

By **Marcellus Allen**

BLOOD OF A BOSS **V**

By **Askari**

LOYAL TO THE GAME **IV**

LIFE OF SIN II

By **T.J. & Jelissa**

A DOPEBOY'S PRAYER **II**

By **Eddie "Wolf" Lee**

IF LOVING YOU IS WRONG... **III**

LOVE ME EVEN WHEN IT HURTS **II**

By **Jelissa**

TRUE SAVAGE **VII**

By **Chris Green**

BLAST FOR ME **III**

A BRONX TALE III

DUFFLE BAG CARTEL

By **Ghost**

ADDICTIED TO THE DRAMA **III**

By **Jamila Mathis**

LIPSTICK KILLAH **III**

WHAT BAD BITCHES DO **III**

KILL ZONE **II**

By **Aryanna**

THE COST OF LOYALTY **II**

By **Kweli**

SHE FELL IN LOVE WITH A REAL ONE **II**

By **Tamara Butler**

RENEGADE BOYS **III**

By **Meesha**

CORRUPTED BY A GANGSTA **IV**

By **Destiny Skai**

A GANGSTER'S CODE **III**

By **J-Blunt**

KING OF NEW YORK IV

RISE TO POWER II

By **T.J. Edwards**

GORILLAS IN THE BAY II

**De'Kari**

THE STREETS ARE CALLING II

**Duquie Wilson**

KINGPIN KILLAZ III

**Hood Rich**

STEADY MOBBIN' **III**

**Marcellus Allen**

SINS OF A HUSTLA II

**ASAD**

CASH MONEY HOES

**Nicole Goosby**

TRIGGADALE II

**Elijah R. Freeman**

MARRIED TO A BOSS 2...

**By Destiny Skai & Chris Green**

KINGS OF THE GAME II

**Playa Ray**

<u>Available Now</u>

<u>RESTRAINING ORDER **I & II**</u>

By **CA$H & Coffee**

<u>LOVE KNOWS NO BOUNDARIES **I II & III**</u>

By **Coffee**

<u>RAISED AS A GOON I, II, III & IV</u>

<u>BRED BY THE SLUMS I, II, III</u>

<u>BLAST FOR ME I & II</u>

<u>ROTTEN TO THE CORE I III</u>

<u>A BRONX TALE I, II</u>

By **Ghost**

<u>LAY IT DOWN **I & II**</u>

<u>LAST OF A DYING BREED</u>

<u>BLOOD STAINS OF A SHOTTA I & II</u>

By **Jamaica**

<u>LOYAL TO THE GAME</u>

LOYAL TO THE GAME II

LOYAL TO THE GAME III

LIFE OF SIN

By **TJ & Jelissa**

BLOODY COMMAS I & II

SKI MASK CARTEL I  II & III

KING OF NEW YORK I II,III

RISE TO POWER


By **T.J. Edwards**

IF LOVING HIM IS WRONG…I & II

LOVE ME EVEN WHEN IT HURTS

By **Jelissa**

WHEN THE STREETS CLAP BACK I & II III

By **Jibril Williams**

A DISTINGUISHED THUG STOLE MY HEART I II & III

LOVE SHOULDN'T HURT I II III

RENEGADE BOYS I & II

By **Meesha**

A GANGSTER'S CODE I & II

By **J-Blunt**

PUSH IT TO THE LIMIT

By **Bre' Hayes**

BLOOD OF A BOSS **I, II, III & IV**

By **Askari**

THE STREETS BLEED MURDER **I, II & III**

THE HEART OF A GANGSTA I II& III

By **Jerry Jackson**

CUM FOR ME

CUM FOR ME 2

CUM FOR ME 3

CUM FOR ME 4

An **LDP Erotica Collaboration**

BRIDE OF A HUSTLA **I  II & II**

THE FETTI GIRLS **I, II& III**

CORRUPTED BY A GANGSTA I, II & III

By **Destiny Skai**

WHEN A GOOD GIRL GOES BAD

By **Adrienne**

A GANGSTER'S REVENGE **I II III & IV**

THE BOSS MAN'S DAUGHTERS

THE BOSS MAN'S DAUGHTERS II

THE BOSSMAN'S DAUGHTERS III

THE BOSSMAN'S DAUGHTERS IV

THE BOSS MAN'S DAUGHTERS **V**

A SAVAGE LOVE  **I & II**

BAE BELONGS TO ME

A HUSTLER'S DECEIT I, II

WHAT BAD BITCHES DO I, II

By **Aryanna**

A KINGPIN'S AMBITON

A KINGPIN'S AMBITION **II**

I MURDER FOR THE DOUGH

By **Ambitious**

TRUE SAVAGE

TRUE SAVAGE II

TRUE SAVAGE **III**

TRUE SAVAGE **IV**

TRUE SAVAGE **V**

TRUE SAVAGE **VI**

By **Chris Green**

A DOPEBOY'S PRAYER

By **Eddie "Wolf" Lee**

THE KING CARTEL **I, II & III**

By **Frank Gresham**

THESE NIGGAS AIN'T LOYAL **I, II & III**

By **Nikki Tee**

GANGSTA SHYT **I II &III**

By **CATO**

THE ULTIMATE BETRAYAL

By **Phoenix**

BOSS'N UP **I , II & III**

By **Royal Nicole**

I LOVE YOU TO DEATH

**By Destiny J**

I RIDE FOR MY HITTA

I STILL RIDE FOR MY HITTA

By **Misty Holt**

LOVE & CHASIN' PAPER

By **Qay Crockett**

TO DIE IN VAIN

**SINS OF A HUSTLA**

By **ASAD**

BROOKLYN HUSTLAZ

By **Boogsy Morina**

BROOKLYN ON LOCK I & II

By **Sonovia**

GANGSTA CITY

By **Teddy Duke**

A DRUG KING AND HIS DIAMOND I & II III

A DOPEMAN'S RICHES

HER MAN, MINE'S TOO I, II

**By Nicole Goosby**

TRAPHOUSE KING **I II & III**

KINGPIN KILLAZ

By **Hood Rich**

LIPSTICK KILLAH **I, II**

CRIME OF PASSION I & II

By **Mimi**

STEADY MOBBN' **I, II**

By **Marcellus Allen**

WHO SHOT YA **I, II**

**Renta**

GORILLAZ IN THE BAY

**DE'KARI**

TRIGGADALE

**Elijah R. Freeman**

GOD BLESS THE TRAPPERS I, II, III

THESE SCANDALOUS STREETS I, II, III
FEAR MY GANGSTA I, II, III
THESE STREETS DON'T LOVE NOBODY I, II
**Tranay Adams**
THE STREETS ARE CALLING
**Duquie Wilson**
MARRIED TO A BOSS...
**By Destiny Skai & Chris Green**
KINGS OF THE GAME II
**Playa Ray**

## <u>BOOKS BY LDP'S CEO, CA$H</u>

<u>TRUST IN NO MAN</u>

<u>TRUST IN NO MAN 2</u>

<u>TRUST IN NO MAN 3</u>

<u>BONDED BY BLOOD</u>

<u>SHORTY GOT A THUG</u>

<u>THUGS CRY</u>

<u>THUGS CRY 2</u>

<u>THUGS CRY 3</u>

<u>TRUST NO BITCH</u>

<u>TRUST NO BITCH 2</u>

<u>TRUST NO BITCH 3</u>

<u>TIL MY CASKET DROPS</u>

<u>RESTRAINING ORDER</u>

<u>RESTRAINING ORDER 2</u>

<u>IN LOVE WITH A CONVICT</u>

**<u>Coming Soon</u>**

BONDED BY BLOOD 2

BOW DOWN TO MY GANGSTA